Fur Babies and Forgery – A Norwegian Forest Cat Café Cozy Mystery – Book 15

by

Jinty James

Fur Babies and Forgery – A Norwegian
Forest Cat Café Cozy Mystery – Book 15

by

Jinty James

ISBN: 9798768076573

DEDICATION

To my wonderful Mother, Annie,
and AJ

CHAPTER 1

"One, two, three. One, two, three."

Lauren Crenshaw box-stepped to the strains of *The Blue Danube* in the arms of her fiancé, Detective Mitch Denman.

So far, the only thing she liked about their dance lessons was the fact she got to spend extra time with him before the wedding.

"No, no, Lauren." Simone abruptly stopped the classical music. Tall, and slim, her flaming red hair flowed to her shoulders. She wore a long green skirt that whirled around her toned legs when she showed them a waltz movement, and her gauzy, matching top revealed a hint of cleavage.

All Lauren knew about her was that she appeared to be in her forties, and was divorced.

"I thought we were doing well," Mitch whispered in her ear.

"So did I," Lauren replied. She took a moment to appreciate his good looks, and the way his lean, muscular frame filled out his outfit of gray slacks and blue button-down shirt. His dark hair was cut short in anticipation of their wedding day, but not *too* short. His straight nose and dark brown eyes made her heart sigh every time she saw him.

It wasn't just his appearance that attracted her to him. His appreciation of her as a person, and of her independence, was one of the key factors in their relationship.

"Like this." Simone swept in front of Lauren, and took Mitch's hand into her own. "Zoe, turn the music back on."

Lauren's cousin, and right hand in their café, reluctantly obeyed. She and her boyfriend Chris were sharing the lessons. Since Zoe was her co-maid of honor, and Chris was Mitch's best man, it made sense that they find a dance instructor together.

Or so Lauren had thought.

"This is how you do it," Simone tossed over her shoulder as she led Mitch into the romantic waltz.

Going by the expression on his face, Mitch did not seem to think it was as romantic as their teacher did.

"That's what you and Mitch were doing!" Zoe stage-whispered.

"I thought you two looked good," Chris offered. He worked as a paramedic and was an old friend of Mitch's. He too, wore slacks, and a cream button-down shirt.

"I think you'd better cut in." Zoe nudged her, looking a little critical in an outfit of capris and red t-shirt that flattered her slim figure. "I do *not* like the way she's looking at Mitch."

"Neither do I." Lauren frowned. At this very moment, Simone definitely looked like a cougar, eyeing Mitch as if he were the tastiest man she'd seen in a while.

"I think Lauren and I should try it." Mitch disentangled himself from Simone as Lauren approached them.

"Very well." Simone shrugged carelessly. "Zoe and Chris, I want to see better footwork." She stalked back to her phone, which lay on a stool.

3

Lauren felt reassured once she was back in Mitch's arms. Not for the first time, she questioned their choice of dance teacher. But with all the wedding planning, running the café with Annie, her silver-gray Norwegian Forest Cat, and Zoe, as well as solving the occasional murder, somehow time had slipped away. She was marrying Mitch in two weeks, and they'd realized recently they needed to brush up on their dance skills.

Simone had been the first instructor with availability at the moment. They'd tried two other teachers first. Now, Lauren wondered if perhaps Simone's attitude toward Mitch and Chris was the reason she had some open slots. Had word gotten around Zeke's Ridge or even further, that Simone was a bit of a man-eater?

The interior of the studio was plain – wooden walls and floorboards, with a large shelf in a far corner holding an array of gold trophies of different sizes. When they'd turned up for their first lesson, Simone had proudly pointed to the prizes, and informed them she'd won them all.

Lauren and Mitch danced around the floor, passing Zoe and Chris, who she thought waltzed well together. She caught Zoe's eye, and they smiled at each other.

Simone clapped her hands. "You must practice, practice, practice. In fact—" she glanced appreciatively first at Mitch, then at Chris, "—it might be a good idea for the men to have some private lessons with me."

Lauren's eyes widened. Had Simone just said that?

Zoe opened her mouth in protest, but before she could speak, Chris said, "I don't think that's a good idea. Zoe and I will learn together."

"Just what I was about to say about Lauren and me." Mitch shot his friend a grateful man-to-man look. "Thanks for the offer, Simone, but I think your instruction has really helped us improve. In fact, I don't think we need any more lessons."

"Yeah, I thought we were pretty good today," Zoe said. "*All* of us."

"Me too," Lauren added.

Simone sighed a tad theatrically. "*I* am the teacher. I should know if you need more lessons – or not. If you insist on stepping onto the dance floor ill-prepared, at Lauren's wedding, then …" she shrugged. "Do you really want *your* parents, and Lauren's parents, to see that all of you are not as good as you could be?"

Zoe's lips pressed in a mutinous line, while her brown eyes looked like they were going to—

The studio door burst open.

"We lost!" A girl who looked around twenty rushed in. Her blonde hair was a little disheveled.

"Yeah, you said we'd be guaranteed to win – or at least place," a guy who seemed to be around the same age accused, a scowl on his face. "You said if we—"

Simone clapped her hands again. "This is not the time nor the place," she said brusquely. "As you can see, I have students here."

"One of the judges said our movements in the paso doble were illegal," the girl said indignantly.

"We did it exactly how you taught us," the guy added, his short dark hair spiking up, as if he'd run his hands through it in frustration. "We did it perfectly!"

"Oh, those judges." Simone's laugh grated along Lauren's spine. "Some of them are such old fuddy-duddies, they shouldn't be judging. I think *they* are acting illegally, if they told you that."

The girl looked a little relieved. "We did think it strange."

"Who was it?" A little frown appeared on Simone's unlined – until now – forehead. "Terry? Brian? Roger?"

"No, it was Paul someone." The girl blinked at her.

"Oh – him." Simone's tone was one of dismissal. "You mustn't believe anything *he* says. He's a washed-up ballroom dancer who somehow talked his way into getting onto judging panels. Take no notice of him."

7

"But we lost," the guy reminded her.

"You guaranteed we would win – or at least place," the girl added.

"Make an appointment for another day, and we'll talk it over," Simone promised. "Text me when you're free. I'm in the middle of a lesson right now." She indicated Lauren, Mitch, Zoe, and Chris.

"Oh – sorry." The girl looked a little embarrassed. "We were just so upset – the judge said if it was up to him, he'd disqualify us permanently for our paso doble!"

"You promised us," her partner growled, looking ferocious for a second. "Come on." He pulled his partner out of the studio, banging the door behind them.

A few seconds later, Simone tsked. "Amateurs. I never promised them anything. I said they *might* be able to win – or place – and they just heard what they wanted to hear." She shook her head, her bright red locks brushing her shoulders. "I'm sorry you had to witness that. Now, where were we? We have time for a little more dancing." She looked at the two men. "Why don't I show you, Mitch, and you, Chris, how to lead a woman in the most romantic waltz in the world? Lauren, turn on the music." She moved toward Mitch.

"I'm sorry, but Mitch and I have to go now." Lauren straightened her shoulders in her plum wrap dress.

"Yeah, me and Chris too." Zoe backed her up.

"That's right." Mitch sidestepped Simone and wrapped his arm around Lauren's shoulders.

Chris looked at his watch. "I have to start my shift soon."

Zoe grabbed his hand and peered at the timepiece. "We've got to skedaddle."

"Then we'll meet again on Saturday." Simone looked a little frustrated.

"I don't think that's really—" Chris started.

"You have two more lessons," Simone added quickly. "Remember, you paid me in advance for eight. You should get what you pay for."

Lauren wondered at the time if that had been the best idea, but she hadn't taken dance lessons for years and had no idea if that was standard practice now. She glanced doubtfully at their instructor. Perhaps it wasn't.

"Okay," Mitch replied after a moment. "If we're all agreed."

Zoe shrugged. Lauren nodded reluctantly.

"All right," Chris said.

"Then I'll see you Saturday afternoon," Simone said.

They walked out of the studio into the twilight.

"I'm sorry." Mitch kept his arm wrapped around her. "I don't think we should have hired Simone."

"Yeah," Chris replied with feeling, his even, attractive features twisted in a shadowy grimace. "The way she looks at me sometimes, I feel like I'm a piece of meat, and she's planning on barbecuing me."

"Only I'm allowed to do that." Zoe giggled, then quickly sobered. "Sorry. But I just don't like her."

"Me neither," Lauren admitted.

"Maybe she's one of those women who don't have women friends – they're only interested in men," Zoe pondered.

"You could be right." Mitch nodded.

They got into Mitch's car for the twenty-minute drive back to Gold Leaf Valley, where they all lived.

"I'm starving," Zoe declared as Mitch pulled up outside Lauren's Victorian cottage, attached to the coffee shop. The small town dated from the Gold Rush era, and the quaint clapboard houses were testament to that. Lauren had inherited both properties from her Gramms a few years ago.

Lauren's stomach grumbled in response. "What are we eating tonight?"

When the four of them got together, they usually took it in turns what to choose for dinner.

"I think it's your choice." Mitch switched off the ignition and smiled at her.

She turned her head toward the backseat. "Chris? I thought it might be your turn."

He smiled. "I usually let Zoe choose."

"And that was last week," Zoe added. "Pizza."

"I vote for pizza again." She was pretty sure no one would protest. She was right.

"Awesome!" Zoe grinned.

Lauren led the way into the cottage. All she wanted to do was cuddle her fur baby and relax.

"Brrt!" A large, silver-gray tabby with long fur ran up to her as soon as she unlocked the front door.

"I missed you, too." Lauren picked up Annie and held her close, relishing the velvety soft fur on her fingertips.

She'd spent the day with her at the coffee shop. It was a certified cat café, and Annie worked with her and Zoe, choosing tables for the customers, and spending time with her favorites. Lauren baked the cupcakes and made the lattes, cappuccinos, and mochas, with Zoe helping. But they both knew that Annie was a real draw card and one of the reasons they had so many customers, although their regulars praised the baked goods and coffee.

She'd only been apart from Annie for a couple of hours since they'd closed at five, but for some reason it felt a lot longer. Perhaps it was the dance lesson she hadn't enjoyed that much, apart from being in Mitch's arms, or the fact that with the upcoming wedding, her life was going to change.

"Hi, Annie." Chris smiled at the feline in Lauren's arms.

"Brrt!" *Hi!*

Zoe and Mitch greeted Annie as well, and the five of them made their way to the living room.

"Phew." Zoe flopped onto the pink sofa. "I'm glad that lesson is over."

"Me too," Lauren admitted, easing down next to her, Annie still in her arms. Her fur baby snuggled into her chest, as if she wanted to stay there for a while.

She looked up at Mitch, who smiled down at her and Annie.

"Want me to call for pizza?" he offered.

"Thanks. I'll have the Lauren special."

"And I'll have the Zoe special."

"Sounds good." Chris nodded.

"Don't you have a shift?" Lauren glanced at him.

"In almost two hours." He checked his watch. "I should have just enough time for dinner with you guys. I'd rather spend any free time I have with you than dancing with Simone."

"Good." Zoe smiled at him.

When the pizzas arrived, the guys took them into the kitchen. Annie sat in the middle, between Lauren and Zoe, on one side of the large table. Mitch and Chris took the opposite side.

"I like your special." Zoe helped herself to a large piece.

Lauren nodded, her mouth full. Her "special" consisted of Canadian bacon, sundried tomato, and mushroom.

"You guys should have a special, too," Zoe said.

"But we love yours," Chris told her.

The Zoe special consisted of pepperoni and sausage.

"Brrt?" Annie peered at Lauren's plate. A small piece of crust with Canadian bacon and sundried tomato remained.

"I don't know if pizza is good for cats," she apologized.

"You had your beef in gravy just now," Zoe reminded Annie. "That was yummy, wasn't it?"

"Brrp." Annie looked like she'd welcome some pizza as well.

They talked about their plans for the next few days.

"Dance lessons Saturday afternoon," Chris reminded them.

Zoe wrinkled her nose.

"Are you free on Sunday?" Mitch glanced at Lauren. "We could have lunch together, after church."

"That sounds great." She smiled at him.

"And we can have lunch together too," Zoe suggested to Chris. "Unless you're working?"

"I'm all yours."

"We could go to Gary's Burger Diner." She winked at Lauren. "We don't want to cramp your style."

"Brrp?"

"I'll bring you home a plain patty," Zoe promised Annie.

"Thanks." Lauren smiled at her cousin. Annie loved the burgers from Gary's.

"Brrt!" *Thank you!* Annie bunted Zoe's hand.

"I'm picking up my gown on Monday," Lauren said.

"And my co-maid of honor outfit," Zoe added. "It's lucky the café is closed that day."

After a quick dessert of vanilla ice cream, Chris left to start his shift.

Mitch also departed, saying he was going to pack some more boxes. He lived in a small apartment, which Zoe was going to take over after the wedding.

Annie sat on Lauren's lap, Zoe next to them on the sofa, while they all watched a crime drama – Zoe's pick. Last night it had been Lauren's turn, and they'd viewed a rom-com.

She relished this time with her two best friends, and settled in to enjoy the show.

CHAPTER 2

"Craft club tonight," Zoe reminded Lauren the next morning as they readied the café.

On Friday evenings, the trio visited their friend and regular customer, Mrs. Finch, and took their handicrafts with them. Lauren was frantically knitting a scarf for Zoe for Christmas, while Zoe had just put the finishing touches on the pottery mugs she'd made – her wedding gift to Lauren and Mitch.

Lauren had paid her to make extras for the café – their customers already used Zoe's mugs when they ate in, and also purchased them to use at home. Ms. Tobin, one of their regular customers, owned the complete collection! Each mug featured Annie in a different pose, and the wedding design had the names *Lauren and Mitch* with the wedding date on one side, and Annie wearing her co-maid of honor floral headdress on the other.

"I'm looking forward to it," Lauren replied.

"Brrt!" Annie added from her pink basket. She'd already strolled around the room, as if to check that Zoe had unstacked all the chairs correctly. Now she waited in her basket for their first customer.

The rattle of pastry tins from behind the swinging kitchen doors signaled that Ed, her pastry chef, was hard at work. Lauren prided herself on her cupcakes, but had to admit that Ed was better at making pastry. Everyone raved about his tender, flaky Danishes. Today he was making honeyed walnut, and cherry pinwheels.

On the dot of nine-thirty, Lauren unlocked the glass and oak entrance door.

"I got here just in time." Their friend, Brooke, the local hairdresser, entered. Her chestnut locks were cut in a long bob with feathered ends and had attractive reddish highlights. The hair color flattered her friendly green eyes. She looked neat and efficient in jeans and a green sweater.

"Brrt!" Annie trotted to greet her, as she stood at the *Please Wait to be Seated* sign.

"Hi, Annie." Brooke smiled down at her. "I'm afraid I don't have time to sit at a table today. My first client is arriving in fifteen minutes."

"Brrp." Annie looked disappointed.

"But I can chat with you, and Lauren and Zoe, while I wait for my coffee."

That seemed to cheer up the feline. She led Brooke over to the counter to place her order.

"How's the wedding prep going?" Brooke asked.

"Are you and Jeff having dance lessons for your wedding?" Zoe inquired.

"We've already started, but we're not getting married for a couple of months. You should be getting your invitation soon." She smiled.

"Who's your instructor?" Lauren asked.

"Carol at Zeke's Ridge. We were lucky she had a cancellation."

"I haven't heard of her." Zoe furrowed her brow.

"No," Lauren agreed.

"We hired Simone—" Zoe glanced around the empty room and leaned across the counter anyway, "but we think we made a mistake."

"Oh." Dismay flickered across Brooke's face. "Jeff and I met her when we were deciding, but I didn't like the way she looked at Jeff."

"I know what you mean." Lauren nodded, thinking of how Simone had eyed Mitch yesterday.

"Yeah," Zoe added gloomily.

"How many lessons do you have left?"

"Only two." Zoe brightened. "How about you?"

"We've got seven. Our teacher is great. She has tons of experience competing in ballroom dancing as well as teaching it."

"We contacted two instructors in Sacramento, but they said they were full. I thought maybe we should try someone local, and Simone's name was the first that popped up in my online search." Zoe patted her capris' pocket, where her phone resided.

"We thought we'd better hire Simone since she said she could fit us in right away. But now ..." Lauren sighed.

Brooke made a sympathetic face.

While Lauren ground the beans and steamed the milk for their friend's large latte, they chatted about the black and white tuxedo kitten Brooke and Jeff had adopted when the café had held a kitten adoption day nearly one year ago, for the local animal shelter. Then the talk turned to their upcoming hair appointment with her. As her wedding gift, Brooke was styling Lauren and Zoe's hair, and Lauren was paying her to take care of the others in the wedding party.

"Are you two going on a honeymoon right away?" Brooke asked, when Lauren finished off the latte with a peacock design on the micro foam. The advanced latte art class she and Zoe had taken a while ago had really paid off.

"Yes," Lauren replied.

"To Hawaii." Zoe sounded excited for her.

"I'm picking up my gown on Monday," Lauren told her. "At that bridal shop you recommended."

"And I found the most gorgeous outfit there as well." Zoe grinned. "Wait until you see it!"

"I'll look forward to it. I picked up my wedding dress there last week. It's a mermaid design with beading."

"I bet that will knock Jeff's eyes right out of his head!" Zoe giggled.

They waved goodbye to Brooke, who grabbed a triple chocolate ganache cupcake as well. Annie ambled back to her basket, turned around in a circle and settled down.

A few minutes later, the tap tap of a walking stick alerted them.

"Hi, Mrs. Finch!" Zoe grinned.

"Brrt!" Annie ran to greet her.

"Hello, Annie dear." Mrs. Finch beamed down at the feline. Her gray hair was piled on top of her head in a bun with a couple of wisps escaping, and she wore a beige skirt and white long-sleeved blouse.

"What can we get you?" Lauren smiled.

"A latte please, and one of your lovely cupcakes." The senior peered at the offerings in the glass case. "Is that lavender?"

"Yes."

"That would be perfect."

Annie slowly led Mrs. Finch to a four-seater near the counter, as if she knew her friend couldn't walk very fast.

Lauren and Zoe brought over the order, and sat down for a minute, since there were no other customers to attend to.

"How are your dancing lessons coming along?" Mrs. Finch picked up her cup with wobbly hands, looking at the swan design on top of the micro foam with appreciation.

They told her about yesterday's lesson.

"I'm sorry to hear that." Mrs. Finch looked a little shocked. "I'm afraid I haven't heard of Simone."

"If anyone had, it would be you," Zoe complimented her. Mrs. Finch was a long time local and knew a surprising number of people.

"I wish we had Brooke and Jeff's dance teacher," Lauren said. "She sounds good."

"Yeah." Zoe sighed. "Oh, well. We only have two lessons left."

"Have you chosen the music for your bridal waltz, Lauren?" Mrs. Finch asked.

"It's *The Blue Danube*."

"And it's super traditional, which means it will be super modern!" Zoe giggled.

They chatted to their friend for a couple more minutes, then left Annie to "talk" with her.

Just as they returned to the counter, Ms. Tobin walked in.

"Hi, Ms. Tobin," Zoe greeted her.

"Hello, Zoe, and Lauren."

Ms. Tobin used to be their prickliest customer, but ever since Lauren and

Zoe had saved her from an internet scam, she'd mellowed, and had become one of their most loyal patrons.

Annie brrted an apology to Mrs. Finch, jumped down from her chair, and trotted over to Ms. Tobin.

"Hello, Annie." Ms. Tobin smiled down at the silver-gray tabby.

"Would you like to sit with Mrs. Finch?" Lauren asked. "That way, Annie can spend time with both of you."

"That would be delightful," Ms. Tobin replied.

Mrs. Finch looked up from her lavender cupcake and gave Ms. Tobin a welcoming smile.

After asking for a large latte and a honeyed walnut pastry, Ms. Tobin followed Annie to the table.

"Sometimes I can't believe how much Ms. Tobin has changed," Zoe murmured to Lauren, the grinding noise of the espresso machine in the background.

"I know," Lauren agreed.

"Definitely for the better," Zoe added.

They brought Ms. Tobin's order over to her.

"How's your kitten, Miranda?" Lauren asked. "I guess she's growing up now."

"She's such a darling girl." Ms. Tobin smiled. "I took her to the vet the other day for a general checkup and she said she's in marvelous health. I do appreciate you finding Miranda for me, Annie."

"Brrt," Annie said modestly.

Annie had chosen the orange, brown, and white calico for Ms. Tobin on the same adoption day Brooke and Jeff had found their kitten.

"How's your friend, Miranda?" Lauren asked.

Ms. Tobin had named the kitten after her long-lost childhood playmate. Thinking of her had inspired her to track down her old friend, with happy results.

"She's coming to visit me again next month," Ms. Tobin replied, "after your wedding."

"That's wonderful," Mrs. Finch said.

"We call each other every week," Ms. Tobin replied, "but it will be good to see her again."

More customers trickled in, and Lauren and Zoe returned to their duties.

The day flew by, and before Lauren realized, it was five o'clock.

"It will be nice to relax and talk to Mrs. Finch tonight." Zoe bolted the oak and glass entrance door.

"Yes," Lauren agreed, shutting off the espresso machine. Their last customer had departed a few minutes ago.

"Brrt!" Annie padded around the room, sniffing here and there. The walls were pale yellow, and the furniture consisted of pine tables and chairs. A string-art picture of a cupcake with lots of pink frosting decorated one of the walls – evidence of one of Zoe's hobbies.

Sometimes the feline found an item left behind by a customer, but there didn't seem to be anything lurking on the wooden floorboards today.

"What's Mitch doing tonight?" Zoe asked.

"Working. He says he needs to put in a few more extra hours so he can take a week off for our honeymoon."

"He works a lot. Chris does, too." She sighed.

"I know." Lauren admired her husband-to-be's work ethic. She supposed she was the same with wanting to perfect her cupcakes and coffee.

"What about Detective Castern?" Zoe pressed.

"What about him?" Lauren frowned.

Detective Castern was the only thorn at Mitch's workplace. Mitch was a dedicated detective, but his colleague preferred to arrest people first and ask questions later – and sometimes he slapped the handcuffs on the wrong person.

"Has he made any more boo-boos lately?"

"Not that I know of."

"Maybe he'll retire soon," Zoe said hopefully.

"I think Mitch would like that idea." Lauren hid a smile. "But I'm not sure if Detective Castern is old enough to retire."

"He looks like he is."

"Zoe!"

"Well, he looks over fifty."

"Mmm."

Lauren took care of the dishes in the commercial kitchen while Zoe vacuumed.

"Now we can have a quick dinner, and go to Mrs. Finch's." Zoe led the way through the private hallway that connected the café to the cottage.

She sank down on one of the kitchen chairs and looked expectantly at Lauren. "What are we having?"

"I have no idea." Lauren sat opposite her.

Annie hopped up on Lauren's lap.

"But you usually know what we're having for dinner."

Zoe was not known for her cooking, although sometimes she liked making pizza with a ready-made base.

"We sold out of pides today, otherwise we could have had one each."

"No cupcakes?" Zoe eyed her hopefully.

"I don't think eating cupcakes for dinner with only two weeks until the wedding is a great idea," Lauren replied. As well as cupcakes, they also sold pides with tasty fillings, such as turkey and cranberry.

Since she'd been fitted for her wedding gown, she'd tried to avoid – or cut down – on sweet treats. She thought her success rate had been around seventy-five percent. Not for the first time, she envied her cousin's slim figure. Zoe seemed to be able to eat whatever she wanted and not gain a single ounce, something that was not Lauren's experience.

Mitch told her he loved her curves, but she didn't want to become any curvier, especially before walking down the aisle.

"Pooh." Zoe made a face.

"We could make a tuna salad," Lauren offered. "There's lettuce in the fridge, and cans of tuna in the pantry."

"Brrt!" Annie's ears pricked up at the mention of fish.

Lauren gave Annie her own cat food tuna, while Zoe assembled their healthy salads.

"What are you going to do when you move into Mitch's apartment?" Lauren asked curiously.

"You've already invited me over here for dinner a few nights per week." Zoe grinned. "I guess I'll get pizza the rest of the time – or burgers at Gary's – or make my own pizza." At Lauren's concerned look, she added, "I'll make sure I'll eat some salad as well. Anyway, we'll see each other practically every day at the café."

Lauren nodded. "And craft club Friday nights."

"That's right." Zoe giggled. "In some ways it will be like nothing's changed."

Lauren blinked away sudden tears. They'd been roomies for a few years now, ever since Zoe had visited her from San Francisco after Lauren had inherited the café. What was meant to be a short stay had turned into a permanent one. Lauren had impulsively offered Zoe a full-time job at the café, and her cousin had jumped at the offer. Now they shared Lauren's cottage (luckily it had two bedrooms) and often explored the surrounding area together on their days off.

The situation had worked perfectly for the three of them – including Annie – but after the wedding, things were going to be a little different.

They arrived at Mrs. Finch's house just after seven, twilight surrounding them.

"Hello, dears." Mrs. Finch looked pleased to see them. "Lauren, have you brought your knitting with you?"

"Yes." Lauren held up her yellow craft bag.

They followed their friend down the lilac hall and into the fawn and beige living room.

Mrs. Finch sank into her armchair.

"Are you okay?" Lauren looked at her in concern.

"I'm fine." She waved a wobbly hand in the air. "I'm afraid I might have overdone it a little today – perhaps I shouldn't have come to the café on a craft club day."

"You know Lauren and I can drive you home anytime if you don't feel like walking," Zoe offered.

"Brrt!" Annie agreed. She jumped onto the arm of Mrs. Finch's chair.

"I know, dears, and it's very kind of you. Perhaps one day I'll ask you."

"Of course." Lauren smiled.

Lauren brought out the red and purple scarf she was knitting for Zoe's Christmas present, while Zoe described the pottery mugs she'd made for the wedding.

"And every guest will receive one," she enthused. "And I'm making more for the café as well."

"It all sounds lovely." Mrs. Finch nodded.

"I'm glad we're having the reception at the bistro," Lauren remarked.

"Yeah, the food is always good there, and I love the menu we – Lauren – chose. Mini crab cakes with micro-greens, steak or Tuscan chicken, and chocolate mousse or lemon cheesecake."

"I'm certainly looking forward to it," Mrs. Finch said. "I'm sure you're going to look beautiful in your wedding dress, Lauren, and Zoe, you'll be wearing a maid of honor outfit, won't you?"

"Co-maid of honor." Zoe winked at Annie, who appeared to return the wink.

"Oh, of course. I'm sorry, Annie."

"Brrp." The feline bunted Mrs. Finch's arm as if to say, *That's okay*.

They chatted about all their preparations for the wedding, butterflies flitting around in Lauren's stomach.

Every time she saw Mitch, he took her breath away, even though they'd been engaged for months, and had dated for a while before he'd proposed. She hoped she still felt like that when they were an old married couple.

They made Mrs. Finch a latte before they left. Zoe popped a capsule into the little machine, while Lauren heated the milk.

"Thank you." Mrs. Finch took a sip. "Somehow it always tastes nicer when you girls make it."

They promised to visit Mrs. Finch on Monday.

"I'll bring some more coffee pods, because you're running low," Zoe observed.

"That's very kind." Mrs. Finch beamed at her. "Let me know how much I owe you."

"It's my gift." Zoe waved goodbye when they reached the porch, the dark night sky surrounding them.

"I love craft club." Zoe sighed.
"Me too."
"Brrt!"

CHAPTER 3

Lauren's stomach tightened as she walked toward the dance studio door on Saturday afternoon.

Mitch must have picked up on her tension, because he glanced at her in concern.

"Are you okay?"

She nodded.

"Let's get this over with." Zoe marched ahead of them and opened the door – to stop in her tracks.

"What—?" Lauren nearly bumped into her, but saved herself in time.

"Shh!" Zoe turned around, a finger to her lips.

Lauren, Mitch, and Chris crowded behind her.

"How dare you badmouth me all over town!" An older female voice.

"What? I would never!" Simone sounded outraged.

"I'll have you know that I've been teaching ballroom dancing for years. I've won the trophies in *real* competitions, and put the time in teaching students. I didn't mind when you set up your studio here; I thought we might even become friends – ha! That was before I had my suspicions about you. But I will not have you go around telling everyone I'm a fraud."

"Of course I wouldn't do something like that." Simone sounded sincere, but Lauren started to wonder.

"I've asked my friends who work in Sacramento, who also teach dance, and they've all said they've never heard of you."

"That's because I haven't taught there."

"But they've never heard of you on the competition circuit, either. And this trophy right here – Best Dance Teacher California 2019 – really? Where did you teach in 2019? It wasn't in Zeke's Ridge."

"It was a small town near San Francisco," Simone replied after a second. "My students loved me, and when my lease was up on my studio there, they bought me that trophy and had it inscribed. How could I refuse such a gift?"

"Hmmph. And by the way, I now have two of your former students, the amateur ballroom dancing couple. They showed me their moves in the paso doble, and I'm sorry to say, what you taught them *is* illegal."

Loud footsteps stalked toward the door. The four of them sprang back.

A sixtyish looking woman with short blonde-gray hair, and wearing a sensible black dancing outfit, swept out, not even noticing them.

Lauren looked at Mitch, then Zoe. Zoe looked at Chris.

"Do you think it's safe to go in?" Chris murmured.

"We might as well." Mitch strode inside.

"Oh, Mitch." Simone sounded pleased – perhaps a little too pleased – to see him.

Lauren entered the studio, Zoe and Chris right behind her.

"Good – everyone's here." Simone's voice was suddenly a little brusque. Today she wore an orange flared skirt and gauzy top, but somehow the color didn't clash with her hair.

"What was that all about?" Zoe asked curiously.

"Nothing." Simone shook her head. "I'm sorry if you overheard. Just a disgruntled dance instructor."

"And the young couple who burst in at the end of our lesson on Thursday?" Mitch probed. "*Were* their dance moves illegal?"

"Of course not." Simone tossed her head back, her red locks shimmering across her shoulders, and laughed. "Just another old fuddy-duddy teacher. Listen, I can – and am – teaching you four to dance at Lauren's wedding. I'm up to date with all the latest techniques, which is more than can be said for most of the other teachers in the area. Maybe it's because I'm younger than them and it's easier for me to keep up with new trends – such as the new dancing shoes I ordered for myself."

When no one said anything, Simone continued, "Unlike *some* old-fashioned dance instructors, I like to wear *nice* outfits." She did a little twirl, glancing at Mitch and Chris speculatively, then pointed one sparkly orange high-heeled shod foot toward them.

Lauren wondered if Simone was alluding to the woman they'd overheard arguing with her a few minutes ago.

"My new shoes are arriving by special delivery, and they're white with purple swirls – very expensive, but I just had to have them. In fact, they're scheduled to arrive at six p.m. on the day of your last lesson." Simone gave Mitch and Chris a flirtatious look. "I'll be wearing them when you arrive, and you can see for yourself how wonderful they are.

"Now, let's get started." Simone clapped her hands, and turned on the music.

Lauren told herself to relax and let the strains of the Viennese music wash over her. She and Mitch waltzed around the dance floor, not even getting criticism from Simone. She snuck a peek at their instructor.

Simone suddenly looked distracted as she stared into space.

Zoe cast her a puzzled glance as she swept past with Chris.

Lauren nodded in return. It was most unusual for Simone not to critique their footwork.

The waltz ended, and they paused, waiting for Simone to say something.

Their instructor blinked, seeming to realize the music had stopped.

"Oh. Do it again." She pressed a button on her phone. "Remember your footwork!"

After criticizing Lauren and Zoe three times each, and the guys just once, Simone ended the class.

"Our final lesson will be on Tuesday evening." She frowned. "When is the wedding?"

"In exactly two weeks," Lauren said.

"I can't wait." Mitch wrapped his arm around her waist and smiled down at her.

"Make sure you practice. I can, of course, offer you a few more lessons before your wedding day. I really think you two – all of you—" she glanced at Zoe and Chris, "need to put in a lot more work before the big day." She picked up her phone. "Let's see, I can give you another lesson next Saturday afternoon, and lessons every day the following week—"

"Thanks, but Lauren and I are happy with our progress." Mitch spoke. "Tuesday will be our last lesson."

"Yeah," Zoe and Chris agreed.

"It's up to you," Simone sounded doubtful. "Why don't you think it over?"

Lauren glanced at the gold trophies lined up on a shelf as they left the studio. She hadn't taken a good look before – she didn't want Simone to think she was being nosy – but had Simone's rival been telling the truth? Was it cute that Simone displayed the best dance teacher trophy from her students, or was it a little dishonest if it gave the wrong impression? And how did the rival instructor know what was engraved on that trophy? Had she been close enough to read the wording? Lauren couldn't read the inscription from across the room.

They got into Mitch's car.

"Do you think that was Brooke and Jeff's teacher?" Zoe asked. "The woman arguing with Simone when we arrived?"

"It could be. Brooke said they were having lessons from someone in Zeke's Ridge." Lauren twisted around to stare at her cousin in the back seat.

"We'll have to ask Brooke when we see her again." Zoe sounded intrigued. "Don't you think it's strange there are two dance studios in a small town like Zeke's Ridge, but none in Gold Leaf Valley?"

"Yes," Lauren said.

"Maybe there aren't any studios for rent," Chris said thoughtfully.

"That's true," Zoe said. "I'm lucky I'm getting Mitch's apartment when he moves into the cottage."

There had been a shortage of houses to rent in the town for a while now. Perhaps that was the case for small business premises as well.

Mitch drove them back to Gold Leaf Valley. Chris accompanied Mitch to his apartment to help him pack some more boxes, then they planned to come back in a couple of hours and have dinner with Lauren and Zoe at Gary's Burger Diner, bringing Annie home a plain beef patty.

Lauren looked forward to the next two days – church tomorrow, and picking up her wedding gown on Monday. Surely nothing could go wrong there?

CHAPTER 4

"Hi, Father Mike," Zoe greeted the Episcopalian priest the next morning. Middle-aged and balding, he was beloved by the whole town.

The church service had just ended, and Father Mike was saying goodbye to everyone in front of the cream clapboard church.

"Hi, Zoe. And Lauren, and Mitch, and Chris. It's wonderful to see you all here."

"Thank you," Lauren replied, feeling a little guilty that they were sporadic church-goers. But with the run-up to the wedding, she and Mitch had made a more conscientious effort to attend each week. They were grateful to Father Mike for agreeing to marry them – Lauren didn't think it would be the same if he didn't.

"How's Mrs. Snuggle?" Zoe asked. Earlier that year, they'd cat sat the white Persian when Father Mike had visited Florida for a church conference. He'd adopted the Queen and show cat when her owner had been murdered, since it had been difficult to find her a new home due to her grumpy demeanor.

"I think she might be ready for that video play date with Annie," he replied. "Of course, I understand if you're too busy with all your wedding preparations. It can wait until after your honeymoon – you are having one, aren't you?"

"Of course," Mitch replied. "We're going to Hawaii for a week."

"And I'll be cat sitting Annie," Zoe said. "Or will she be Zoe sitting me?" She giggled.

"Zoe will stay at the cottage with Annie until we return home," Lauren added. "But we'll have time to set up a play date for Mrs. Snuggle and Annie. Just let us know when it's convenient for you."

"What about tomorrow?" Father Mike proposed. "I know it's your day off, so the café will be closed."

"What time are we going to the bridal shop?" Zoe turned to Lauren.

"I thought we could go in the morning, and visit Mrs. Finch on the way home."

"Perfect." Zoe beamed at Father Mike. "We can set up the play date for tomorrow afternoon."

"If you're sure it's not too much trouble," he said.

"Of course not," Lauren replied. "We'll call you after lunch. Is that a good time?"

"Yes." He nodded. "I'll be working on next Sunday's sermon."

"Did the sermon writing workshop you took at the church conference in Florida help a lot?" Zoe asked curiously. "I've always liked your sermons."

"Thank you, Zoe." Father Mike looked pleased. "Yes, the workshop did help, and now they don't take me as long to write, which means I can assist more people who need my help."

They said goodbye to him, and walked back to the cottage.

"We *are* making a wedding donation to the church, aren't we?" Lauren turned to Mitch.

"Definitely." He nodded. "Father Mike said it wasn't necessary, but he does a lot of good in the community and this is one way to thank him."

"If there's any food left over at the reception, maybe we could give it to him," Zoe suggested. "I bet he knows exactly who would appreciate it."

Chris wrapped his arm around her shoulders. "And that's one of the reasons I love you." He kissed the top of her brunette pixie hair.

"Only one?" she teased, her cheeks a faint pink.

He grinned.

Annie ran to greet them when they entered the cottage.

"Mitch and I are having lunch at the vineyard today," she told her fur baby.

"And Chris and I are going to Gary's."

"You went there last night," Lauren teased.

"That's how much I love the burgers." Zoe grinned. "I'll bring you back a plain patty, Annie."

"Brrt!" *Thank you.*

Lauren played with Annie and her jingly ball before they left for the winery.

Thirty minutes later, when she was relaxing with Mitch in the outdoor café at the vineyard, a thought struck her.

"I forgot to tell Annie about her cyber play date with Mrs. Snuggle on Monday."

"It will be a surprise for her." Mitch smiled. "A pleasant one, I hope."

"Annie likes to make friends with everyone, but she seems to sense when someone isn't interested, whether it's a human or another cat. Maybe Mrs. Snuggle is interested in being friends with her now."

"She certainly is a special cat." Mitch captured her hand across the white metal table. "And her mom is special, too."

"Ohh." Lauren's eyes became misty. When she'd first met Mitch, he'd been inexperienced with cats, and hadn't been sure what to make of Annie. Now, the two of them were good friends, and Annie seemed to accept him as part of their life.

"Does Annie know we're going to Hawaii?" he asked.

"I've mentioned it in general terms to her, but I'm not sure if she realizes we're leaving straight after the wedding. I'll have to start telling her, and show her the travel brochures."

"Good idea. I'm sure she'll be okay with Zoe looking after her."

"Yes." Lauren nodded. "And Zoe will send me live updates on her phone so Annie and I will be able to see and talk to each other."

"Good." He brought her hand to his lips.

Lauren enjoyed her lunch with Mitch. It was great to have some one-on-one time together. What with all the wedding planning, dance lessons, and hanging out a lot with Zoe and Chris – which she loved – it made her appreciate having couple time even more.

When they returned to the cottage, Zoe and Chris were already relaxing in the living room, watching a spy drama with Annie.

"You mean you aren't watching the movie about the princess who discovers her whole life is a lie?" Lauren teased.

"Brrt!" *Apart from being a princess!*

"Annie said I could choose." Zoe grinned.

"Yeah," Chris agreed, amusement on his face.

"I'm sure Annie will want to watch that movie – and it's great – again soon," Zoe said.

Lauren sat down on the older sofa, covered with a pink slip cover to match their newer one. Annie trotted over to her and jumped into her lap.

"You can choose the next show," Lauren told her.

"Brrt." *Thank you.*

Mitch joined them on the sofa. "Can you catch us up?" he glanced at Chris.

Lauren settled down to enjoy the drama. She thought Annie did too,

even though it wasn't the princess
movie.

CHAPTER 5

On Monday morning, Lauren yawned as she crunched granola. They'd all stayed up a little later than usual watching the rest of the spy drama episodes. If she didn't have errands that morning, she would have slept late for once.

"We must go to bed earlier tonight. And every night until the ceremony, I guess." Zoe slathered butter onto her whole- wheat toast. "We don't want to have bags under our eyes on your wedding day."

"Brrt," Annie agreed. She'd just finished her chicken in gravy, and hopped up on the chair next to Lauren's.

"We're picking up my wedding gown today," she told her fur baby.

"And then we're visiting Mrs. Finch," Zoe added. "We've got to stop at the grocery store on the way and pick up some more coffee pods for her."

Lauren nodded. "And then, Father Mike thought Mrs. Snuggle might be ready for a video play date with you," she told Annie. What do you think?"

"Brrt!" *Good!*

"You can show her your toys, and I'm sure she'll show you hers," Lauren continued.

"I'm positive she appreciated you looking after her when Father Mike went to Florida for his church conference in January," Zoe added.

"Brrp." Annie bunted Lauren's arm.

They finished breakfast, said goodbye to Annie, and drove to Sacramento in Lauren's white compact car.

"Are you going to try on your gown one more time?" Zoe asked.

"I guess." Since she hadn't been married before, she wasn't quite sure what the correct etiquette was.

"Did you show your mom a photo of it?"

"Of course." Lauren nodded. Her parents lived in Sacramento and were paying for most of the wedding, including her dress, something

Lauren appreciated a great deal. So did Mitch.

Her mother had offered to accompany Lauren dress shopping, but seemed to understand when Lauren had explained she'd like to share the experience with Zoe. She loved her mother, but sometimes she seemed to discover Lauren's figure flaws easily.

"I can't wait to try on my outfit again." Zoe giggled. "I just love it. Thank you for letting me choose what I wanted." Her tone became serious.

"You're welcome. What sort of person would I be if I asked you to wear something you weren't comfortable in?"

"I know, but you know how some brides become monsters. Like Brianna, that bride-to-be we met weeks ago when we were checking out Stately Vue Hall for your reception." Zoe tapped her cheek. "Are she and Bobby still together?"

"As far as I know," Lauren replied. "Mitch hasn't mentioned anything."

"Hmm." Zoe stared out of the window, the trees rushing past them.

They arrived at the bridal store, featuring a strapless gown with detailed beading in the window. A bell tinkled overhead as they opened the door.

"Lauren." Celeste, the manager, smiled. "And Zoe. Wonderful! I have your outfits ready. Would you like to try them on to make sure everything fits perfectly?"

"Yes!" Zoe hurried over to her elegant pantsuit and held it against herself.

"That is so you." Lauren admired the co-maid of honor outfit.

"And I'll be wearing a floral headband with cat safe flowers."

Lauren nodded. "The florist confirmed last week that the headband will contain gerberas, little roses, and orchids."

"And your cat Annie is the other maid of honor, isn't she?" Celeste smiled. "What a darling idea."

"We think so." Zoe giggled.

Zoe tried on her outfit first. She came out of the changing room, her face alight. "What do you think?"

She twirled around in long pants in the palest of champagne, with a sleeveless matching top, tied together with a wide sash that flared with the movement.

"You look amazing," Lauren said truthfully.

"Thanks." Zoe smoothed her hand down her left pants' leg. "I just love this fabric. It feels so – so – perfect and soft."

It wasn't like Zoe to be lost for words.

"Your shoes have come in," Celeste told her.

Zoe beamed, and immediately slipped on the champagne ankle strap pumps with a modest heel. She walked on the carpet for a few seconds. "Perfect!"

"Now it's your turn." Zoe turned to her. "Go and try on your dress. I can't wait to see you in it!"

Lauren took her turn in the changing room. When she looked at herself in the full-length mirror, she couldn't stop smiling.

"Well?" Zoe called eagerly. "Have you got it on yet? Can we see?"

"You've seen it before." Lauren slowly walked out in an ivory satin gown with a sweetheart neckline that flattered her curves. She'd spied the dress through the boutique window a couple of months ago, and it had been the first gown she'd tried on – and fallen in love with.

"Oh – you look beautiful," Celeste said.

"Yeah – you do." Zoe smiled at her. "I can't believe you're getting married!"

"I know. I feel like I should pinch myself."

"I'll do it." Zoe zipped over to her and gently pinched Lauren's arm.

"Ouch!"

"I did try to be careful." Zoe looked remorseful.

"I know." Lauren touched her cousin's arm.

"We're still here in the bridal shop, aren't we? You're not dreaming?"

"No." Lauren shook her head. "I'm not dreaming."

Celeste urged her to give a little twirl and to walk around the shop, to make sure the length of the dress was correct.

"I brought my shoes with me." Lauren sank down onto the plush, padded circular sofa and slipped on her new ivory kitten heels.

"Now you can pretend to walk down the aisle to meet Mitch." Zoe giggled.

"I will." Lauren's eyes grew misty as she slowly walked around the shop, imagining Mitch waiting for her. Sometimes she still couldn't believe she was going to marry him – and in two weeks!

"You're very graceful, Lauren," Celeste praised. "Some of my brides think they need to gallop down the aisle before the groom changes his mind."

"That definitely won't happen with Mitch," Zoe said in all seriousness. "They're in *love.*"

"What about you, Zoe?" Celeste asked. "Do you have a special someone?"

"His name is Chris." Lauren couldn't resist jumping in for once. "And he's a great guy."

"Thanks." Zoe looked pleased at the compliment. "Yeah, he is pretty special."

"Maybe it will be your turn soon," Celeste suggested.

Zoe blushed but remained uncharacteristically silent.

Lauren paid the balance for her gown, knowing her mom would reimburse her. Zoe had already paid for hers – she'd insisted on that point, saying she wanted to help out.

"Have you been taking dance lessons?" Celeste asked, just as they were about to leave.

"Yes, with a teacher called Simone," Lauren answered.

"It's our last lesson tomorrow – thank goodness," Zoe added.

"Oh, dear." Celeste looked a little alarmed. "She hasn't tried to steal your men, has she?"

"No." Lauren's eyes widened. "Well, not really."

"Apart from offering them *private* lessons. But Chris and Mitch turned her down right away."

"Good." Celeste nodded. "It sounds like you both have keepers."

"What have you heard?" Zoe asked curiously.

"Not much, really," Celeste replied hastily. "Just a few mutterings here and there from some of my brides – apparently Simone has moved around California quite a lot."

"We heard that she taught near San Francisco two years ago," Lauren said uncomfortably, their eavesdropping incident flashing through her mind.

"And her students gave her a trophy saying, Best Dance Teacher California 2019," Zoe added. "I lived in San Francisco before then, but I'd never heard of her – not that I investigated dance lessons when I lived there."

"Hmm." Celeste sounded a little doubtful. "Well, I'm sure everything will go smoothly with your bridal waltz."

"I hope so," Lauren replied, realizing that she and Mitch hadn't been practicing much, apart from the actual lessons.

"Maybe we can practice tonight." Sometimes it was as if Zoe read her mind. "If the guys can't make it, we can dance with each other."

"And take turns leading." Lauren stifled a smile.

They said goodbye to Celeste and carefully carried their outfits to the car parked nearby.

"We'd better add dance practice to our list for today." Zoe buckled her seatbelt. "After Mrs. Finch, Mrs. Snuggle—"

"And doing some cupcake prep for tomorrow," Lauren added.

She made sure she stuck to the speed limit all the way home. They made a quick stop at the grocery store for Mrs. Finch's coffee pods, then parked outside her house.

"Let's show Mrs. Finch our bridal outfits," Zoe suggested.

"Good idea." Lauren smiled.

Mrs. Finch greeted them at the front door, and genuinely oohed and ahhed over Lauren's gown and Zoe's co-maid of honor outfit.

"You both will look so beautiful." She dabbed at her eyes. "I can't wait to see you walk down the aisle, Lauren, and you too, Zoe. Will Annie be on her lead?"

"Yes," Lauren replied. "Zoe will accompany her."

"Maybe Annie and I should practice, so we walk in step," Zoe suggested.

"That's a great idea." Lauren smiled. "You two are going to be amazing."

"So are you." Now it was Zoe's turn to look a little misty-eyed.

They made Mrs. Finch a latte with the new capsules, then explained about Annie's cyber play date with Mrs. Snuggle that afternoon.

She shooed them away, saying she would pop into the café tomorrow or the next day.

"I'd better put walking down the aisle practice with Annie on my to do list," Zoe said on the way home.

"The list that is constantly growing."

"And it's only Monday! Imagine how long it will be by the end of the week."

"I don't want to." But right now, nothing could spoil Lauren's good mood. In fact, she'd never been happier.

CHAPTER 6

"Hi, Father Mike," Lauren greeted the priest that afternoon, speaking into her cell phone.

"Hi, Lauren." The priest peered at them through the screen. "I've tried to explain to Mrs. Snuggle what's going to happen, but she's never done this before."

"Annie's quite experienced," Lauren replied. "She's had plenty of video play dates with her friends AJ, and Toby."

"That's good." Father Mike chuckled.

"Annie, are you ready to show Mrs. Snuggle your toys?" Lauren propped the phone up against the leg of the coffee table.

"Brrt!" Annie hopped down from the sofa and batted an orange ball with her paw.

Jingle.

Lauren heard Father Mike say, "Mrs. Snuggle, Annie would like to play with you now. On the phone."

"Meow." A grumpy white Persian face filled the screen, her expression softening when she spotted Annie.

"Brrt." Annie trotted over to the phone.

"Meow." She sounded more welcoming.

"Do you want to show Annie your new toy?" Father Mike said in the background. "It's a fish that makes a crackly noise."

Crinkle crackle came over the device.

"Brrp." Annie sounded encouraging.

"Meow?"

Jingle. Annie batted her ball again.

Lauren smiled to herself as she sank onto the sofa. Perhaps she should keep Annie company, since this was a new way of playing for Mrs. Snuggle.

Reaching for a notepad and pen, she decided to make a start on her wedding cupcake list. Instead of hiring a baker to make an expensive cake, she'd decided to make a cupcake tower, with Zoe's encouragement. She wished she could make a lot of different flavors to please everyone, but she'd finally decided to offer just one – a simple vanilla cake with vanilla frosting and pink fondant flowers. She hoped everyone would understand, and enjoy her creation.

"Brrt!" Annie waved a paw toward the phone.

"Meow."

Lauren saw the Persian's paw wave back tentatively at Annie.

"How's the play date going?" Zoe entered the room. "Hi, Mrs. Snuggle." She smiled encouragingly at the fluffy white cat filling the screen.

"Meow." The Persian sounded almost friendly.

"I thought when Annie and Mrs. Snuggle have finished playing, we can start practicing our co-maid of honor march down the aisle."

"Good idea." Lauren glanced at her fur baby, who rolled her orange ball in front of the phone, waiting for Mrs. Snuggle to pat her fish that made the crinkle crackle noise.

"I texted Chris but he's got a shift tonight." Zoe made a face.

"Do you want me to check if Mitch is free for dance practice, or do you want it to be just the two of us this evening?" Lauren turned to her cousin.

"Just us."

"It'll be fun." Lauren smiled.

After Annie's play date was finished, and they said goodbye to Mrs. Snuggle and Father Mike over the phone, Zoe fetched Annie's harness, and the two of them explained to the feline about practicing walking in time with Zoe.

"Brrt!" Annie's green eyes sparkled in anticipation. She stood patiently while Lauren buckled a lavender harness on her.

"Why don't you two walk down the hall?" Lauren suggested.

"And then you follow us," Zoe told her.

"Okay."

Zoe hummed Mendelssohn's *Wedding March* as she and Annie strolled down the hallway. At first,

Annie was in the lead, as that was how she was used to walking in the harness, but when Zoe stopped and mimed walking perfectly in step with her, Annie seemed to understand. After a couple of tries, they were flawlessly in step, Annie by Zoe's side.

"You're amazing, Annie," Lauren spoke as she followed them down the "aisle". "What you're doing is just perfect." Unbidden tears rose to her eyes – was it normal for brides to be so misty-eyed before the big day?

"Brrt!" *Thank you.* Annie stopped and turned around, her mouth tilting up in a little smile.

"Maybe we should practice again just before the wedding while we wear our floral headbands," Zoe mused.

"Good idea." Lauren nodded.

"Brrt!"

They strolled down the aisle a few more times, then played with Annie for a while. When Lauren checked her practical white wristwatch, she realized she'd forgotten to mix up cupcake batter for the morning. For once, she'd leave it until the next day.

That evening, Lauren and Zoe waltzed around the room. Zoe found the music online, and Annie watched with wide eyes as they took turns leading.

After a couple of mis-steps, Lauren thought they were doing pretty well.

"We're amazing!" Zoe's cheeks were a little flushed at the end of the dance.

"I wouldn't go that far but …"

"We're pretty good."

"Brrt!"

"It's a shame the guys aren't here," Lauren said. "I think Simone was right when she said we should practice a lot before the big day."

"I think that's the only thing she *has* been right about." Zoe frowned.

"Maybe we should dance together at our last lesson with Simone tomorrow," she suggested.

"Good idea – as long as she doesn't want to dance with Chris."

"Or Mitch."

CHAPTER 7

"I can't open the door." Zoe rattled the handle.

They were attempting to enter the dance studio for their last lesson with Simone.

"Want me to try?" Lauren joined her. She twisted and turned the doorknob, frowning.

Mitch and Chris had remained in the car for a minute, talking about which pocket in his suit Chris should carry the wedding rings. He was taking his best man duties very seriously.

The sun had set and shadows were lengthening. There weren't many passersby in the little street.

"Maybe it needs some oomph." Zoe pressed her shoulder to the wooden door. "Got it." She pushed open the door. "It must have gotten stuck."

"Where's Simone?" Lauren crinkled her brow. Usually, their instructor was ready and waiting for them, the strains of *The Blue Danube* playing. Today, the studio was silent and—

"There she is!" Zoe's voice hitched in an indrawn breath on the last word.

Their dance instructor lay on the floor, wearing one of her usual outfits, a long skirt with a gauzy top, and the new shoes she'd boasted about at their last lesson – white with gaudy purple swirls. She also wore a gold trophy stuck on top of her head, which said, Best Dance Teacher California, 2019.

***

"Lauren?" Mitch called from the doorway.

She turned to face him, chewing her lip. "Something's happened to—"

"Let me see." He strode over to the instructor and bent down.

"Do you need me over there?" Chris took a few steps toward Mitch and Simone.

"Not this time." Mitch shook his head. "She's dead." He straightened and moved away from the body. "I'll have to call it in."

"What happened?" Chris asked in a low voice as Mitch spoke on his phone.

Zoe told him, leaning into him a little when he wrapped an arm around her.

"Are you okay, Lauren?" Chris asked.

"I'll be fine." She didn't feel it, though.

"Castern's coming." Mitch sounded frustrated.

"Not him." Zoe made a face.

"Yeah." Mitch ran a hand through his hair. "We'd better wait outside." He took Lauren's hand, his strong fingers comforting around hers. "Are you all right?" he asked her softly.

"I will be." She attempted to smile at him.

"I'm sorry this is happening now – with the wedding less than two weeks away." He grimaced.

"Me too."

They stood outside the studio, waiting for reinforcements.

Detective Castern arrived quickly, barely greeting Mitch, let alone the rest of them, before stalking into the studio.

"Did you see the trophy on Simone's head?" Zoe whispered. "It looked like someone had shoved it onto her scalp." She glanced at Mitch. "Is that how she died? Did someone hit her over the head with it?"

"It looks like she suffered a heavy blow to her head, based on the trickle of blood I saw," Mitch answered. "But we won't know for sure until she's been examined. I didn't want to touch anything."

Lauren nodded in understanding and squeezed his hand. He squeezed hers in reply.

"Denman." Detective Castern followed the crew wheeling out Simone, encased in a black body bag. "What are you doing here?"

Mitch briefly explained about their dance lessons.

"They're getting married," Zoe put in.

Detective Castern grunted. "Were you all together?" He glanced at the four of them.

Mitch explained that Lauren and Zoe had gone ahead while he and Chris stayed in the car for a couple of minutes.

After the detective grudgingly took their statements, he told all of them not to leave town.

"Are you serious?" Mitch demanded. "We work in the same office. Where would I go?"

"Should we postpone our honeymoon?" Lauren asked.

"You might have to." Detective Castern did not look unhappy at that thought. "Denman will be leaving us short- staffed while you two jet off to wherever it is you're going, anyway."

"They're going to Hawaii," Chris told him. "And I don't see how you can stop them, when they're totally innocent."

"That's right." Zoe swept out a hand, encompassing Chris and herself. "We all are."

"I'll be the judge of that," Detective Castern snapped. He shoved his notebook in his jacket pocket and stalked to his car.

"Wow," Zoe said under her breath when he departed. "I'm glad I don't work with him."

"You're lucky," Mitch replied.

"I'm sure we'll be able to postpone the honeymoon if we need to," Lauren reassured him.

"About that—" Mitch cleared his throat. "I found a special deal – it had everything we decided on, but the price was cheaper because it was non-refundable. I'd already had my leave cleared, and we'd set the date, and everything was arranged, but—"

"Then we'll have to solve the murder!" Zoe's brown eyes lit up. "I doubt Detective Castern will do it before the wedding, don't you?"

"Zoe," Chris began to speak.

"You two are going to Hawaii," Zoe said fiercely. "You're going to have an incredible wedding and an even better honeymoon, and I'll look after

Annie. And nothing is going to change that."

Lauren wished Detective Castern could see the expression on Zoe's face. She imagined him standing up straight and saluting her.

"If you put it like that…" Lauren began.

"I was already going to ask my boss if he could give me this case," Mitch said.

"You know I'll do whatever I can to help," Chris added.

"Good!" Zoe smiled. "And I know Annie will help as well."

Lauren imagined her fur baby saying, "Brrt!"

***

The four of them returned to the cottage.

"Can we order something to eat?" Chris looked hopeful. "I'm afraid I didn't have time to get something before we went over to the studio."

"Same here." Mitch nodded.

They decided on pizza, since Gary's Burger Diner didn't deliver. It arrived quickly and they ate Lauren and Zoe specials at the kitchen table, Annie joining them.

Lauren had quickly explained to her fur baby what had happened when they got home, glossing over the distressing bits.

"First thing tomorrow, I'll ask my boss if I can work the case," Mitch said. "Hopefully he'll agree, because sometimes I catch a look on his face after he's dealt with Castern."

"Good." Zoe nodded.

"What about that ballroom dancing couple who burst in during one of our lessons?" Lauren asked.

"Yeah, the girl said Simone taught them an illegal paso doble or something." Zoe wrinkled her brow. "I wonder what that is."

"It's a Latin ballroom dance," Chris said.

They all looked at him.

"What? I looked it up afterward."

"I think it's cool you did that." Zoe rested her head on his arm for a moment.

Instead of the girls sitting on one side of the table and the guys on the other, tonight they sat couple opposite couple, Annie on Lauren's other side.

"There's also that other instructor at our second last lesson on Saturday," Mitch reminded them.

"Oh, yeah." Zoe's eyes widened. "Didn't she accuse Simone of telling people she was a fraud?"

"That's right." Chris nodded.

"So I've got three viable suspects already," Mitch stated.

"What do you mean *you*?" Zoe narrowed her eyes. "I think you mean *we*."

"Zoe," Lauren broke in, "we should let Mitch do his job."

"You have to say that because you're marrying him in less than two weeks. Right?" The look on Zoe's face made it seem very important that Lauren gave the correct answer.

"Brrt!" Annie interrupted them in a scolding tone.

"I'm sorry," Lauren apologized to her fur baby. "You're right. We shouldn't be arguing." She stroked the silver-gray tabby's shoulder.

"Sorry, Annie," Zoe said in a subdued tone.

"Yeah," Mitch added.

Chris nodded.

"This is supposed to be a happy time – for all of us." Lauren glanced at the four of them, including Annie. "Mitch and I are getting married and—"

"And it *will* be a happy time," Zoe promised fiercely.

"Yes. I'm sure if Mitch gets the case, he'll solve it before the wedding." Chris spoke.

"I'll do whatever I can to make that happen," Mitch vowed.

CHAPTER 8

The next morning, Lauren tried to keep it together as she made lemon poppyseed cupcakes, and super vanillas. She set a few aside for Mitch and Chris, and offered one to Ed.

"Thanks," her pastry chef replied with a brief smile. With monster rolling pins for arms and unruly short auburn hair, he was a man of few words, but had a good heart.

"How's AJ?" Lauren asked, referring to his Maine Coon.

Annie had found AJ in the backyard as a tiny, abandoned brown tabby, with a darker brown M on her forehead. Ed and AJ had bonded instantly, turning him into a proud cat papa.

"She's good." He smiled. "I think Annie told her about the wedding during their last play date."

Lauren smiled, imagining the feline conversation, before her thoughts drifted to the previous day.

After Annie had scolded them last night, the evening had ended amicably. Mitch and Chris left before it got too late, as they both had early starts. Mitch promised to update her about the case as soon as he could.

Taking the cupcakes to the counter, she suddenly realized she'd forgotten to tell Mitch something last night.

"What?" Zoe asked curiously. She paused counting the cash in the register before they opened for the day.

"Remember what Celeste, the manager of the bridal shop, told us about Simone?"

"That's right!" Zoe's eyes widened. "She asked us if Simone had stolen Mitch and Chris from us."

"She might be a good person for Mitch to talk to," Lauren mused.

"Or we could talk to her!" Excitement flickered across Zoe's face. "We could grill her!"

"She seems a nice lady," Lauren reminded her. "And she was very helpful to us when we shopped there for our wedding outfits."

"True." Zoe sobered.

They finished getting the café ready for their first customers.

This morning, Ed had made apricot, and blueberry Danishes, and was working on apple and walnut.

"Hi, Ms. Tobin," Lauren greeted their first customer a few minutes after they'd unlocked the door.

"Hello, girls." Ms. Tobin smiled.

"Brrt!" Annie trotted over to greet her.

"How are the wedding preparations coming along? I heard this morning that your dance teacher was killed."

"You heard already?" Zoe's eyes widened.

"The senior center?" Lauren guessed.

"Yes." Ms. Tobin nodded. "My friend helps out there, and called me this morning when she heard. I don't know how she found out, though."

"Maybe one of the members has a police scanner or is retired from the force," Zoe suggested.

"You could be right," Ms. Tobin agreed.

After giving them her order of a large latte and lemon poppyseed cupcake, she followed Annie to a four-seater near the counter.

Annie hopped up onto the chair opposite her, and proceeded to "chat" to her in a series of brrts and brrps.

"Maybe Annie is telling her about practicing her co-maid of honor walk down the aisle," Zoe mused.

"Probably." Lauren glanced fondly at her fur baby before steaming the milk for the latte. When she finished off the beverage with a peacock design, she took it over to Ms. Tobin.

"Thank you." Ms. Tobin looked approvingly at the latte art. "Your peacocks and swans are excellent."

"Thanks." Lauren smiled.

"Oh, before I forget." Ms. Tobin glanced at all of them as Zoe presented the cupcake. "I've bought Annie a little present to celebrate her being co-maid of honor. I heard she donated her gift from you to the animal shelter, so I wanted to make sure she had a little something for herself."

"That's very kind of you." Lauren smiled.

"Definitely." Zoe nodded.

"Brrt!" *Thank you.* Annie sat up straight and seemed to smile at Ms. Tobin.

"I've also bought your gift from the registry list, Lauren."

"Thank you." She meant it.

"What is it?" Zoe asked curiously.

"Zoe!"

"I'm happy to tell you now," Ms. Tobin replied, a little twinkle in her eye. "Unless you'd rather it be a surprise."

"Tell her now," Zoe urged. "After last night, I think we – Lauren – needs to hear something nice."

"Oh, of course." Ms. Tobin sobered. "You found your teacher – Simone – didn't you?"

"Unfortunately." Lauren nodded.

"Well, why don't I tell you what I bought? It's the pink and white plaid blanket."

"That's awesome!" Zoe's face lit up. "Lauren bought one for me as my co-maid of honor gift and I just love it. I made her add it to the registry list so hopefully we would both own one – and be twins!"

"Then I'm doubly glad I purchased it." Ms. Tobin looked amused.

"That's very kind of you," Lauren told their friend.

"Brrt!"

"And I'm going to make a donation to the animal shelter as well." Ms. Tobin took a sip of her latte. "I almost forgot to mention that."

"I'm sure the shelter will appreciate it," Zoe said.

"Brrt!"

"What are you going to do about your dance lessons?" Ms. Tobin asked after a moment.

"Last night was our final one," Lauren replied.

"Thank goodness," Zoe said with feeling, then seemed to realize what she'd said. "Oops. I'm sorry Simone is dead, but she did seem to be a bit of a cougar."

Lauren nodded.

"What did she do?" Ms. Tobin's eyes sharpened.

They quickly told her about Simone's offer of private lessons – for the guys.

Ms. Tobin tutted. "I'm sorry to hear that." She paused. "Do you think you'll try to find another instructor before the big day?"

"We'd thought of just practicing at home," Lauren replied.

"On Monday night Lauren and I waltzed together."

"It was fun." Lauren smiled.

"But maybe we *should* try to find another teacher." Zoe turned to her. "Just to make sure we're as good as we think we are."

"It couldn't hurt," Ms. Tobin said.

"Brrt," Annie agreed.

"I know!" Zoe tapped her cheek. "We could ask Brooke for her teacher's phone number."

"Oh, yes, Brooke is getting married soon, isn't she?" Ms. Tobin patted her brown hair. "I quite enjoy going to her salon."

More customers trickled in and they excused themselves. Annie greeted each one and showed them to a table, before returning to Ms. Tobin. Lauren and Zoe made cappuccinos, lattes, and mochas, as well as plating the sweet treats.

Just before the lunch rush, their friend Hans entered. He was in his sixties and dapper, with gray hair and faded blue eyes.

"Brrt!" Annie ran up to him.

"Hello, *Liebchen*." He bent stiffly to pet her.

"Hi, Hans," Lauren greeted him, a smile on her face.

"Hello, Lauren, and Zoe. It is your wedding day soon."

"And she can't wait!" Zoe giggled.

"Neither can I," she said more seriously. "Annie and I are co-maids of honor."

"So I have heard." There was a twinkle in his eye. "I am looking forward to the big day. But what is this I hear about your dancing teacher? Is it true?"

They quickly filled him in.

"Ach! That is terrible." He shook his head.

After giving them his order of a large cappuccino and blueberry Danish, he followed Annie to a small table near the counter. Annie walked slowly, as if she knew he couldn't hurry.

"I'd better call Brooke and ask for her dance teacher's number." Zoe dug her phone out of her jeans' pocket.

A couple of minutes later she ended the call, just as Lauren had finished making Hans' cappuccino.

"Got it." She put her phone away. "I can take that to Hans." Zoe headed over to his table, carrying a tray with the beverage and pastry.

"Brooke has recommended her instructor to us," Zoe told him.

"I hope she has some open spots." Lauren followed her.

"Only one way to find out." Zoe pulled out her phone. After the short conversation finished, she smiled at the three of them.

"Carol can squeeze us in tonight," Zoe told them.

"Tonight?" Lauren stared at her.

"I know it's short notice, but your wedding *is* only one and a half weeks away."

"I'd better see if Mitch can make it." Lauren fished out her phone.

"I hope Chris doesn't have a shift." Zoe's thumbs got busy.

When they'd finished, there was a smile on both their faces. Hans looked amused.

"Mitch can make it."

"So can Chris."

They high-fived each other.

"Sorry, Hans," Lauren apologized.

"There is no need." His faded blue eyes twinkled. "It's nice that you have good news. I'm sure all of you will be wonderful on the dance floor."

"I hope so," Lauren replied. With all the wedding guests watching them, including her parents – she just hoped she wouldn't mis-step – or worse – stumble, and—

"You're going to be amazing waltzing with Mitch." Zoe broke into her anxious thoughts.

"Brrt!" Annie agreed.

"Thanks." She shook her head slightly to clear it. "I guess I'd better get back to the counter." She spotted two more customers entering.

Annie greeted the newcomers, then returned to Hans, one of her favorite people.

The rest of the day passed smoothly. More of their regulars came in, and by the time it was five o'clock, all the baked goods had sold out.

Zoe eyed the empty glass case mournfully.

"No cupcakes for dinner. What are we eating?"

"I have no idea," Lauren replied truthfully. "But not pizza." If she ate pizza every night, there was the slight possibility she might not fit into her wedding gown on the big day.

"I guess we can munch on salad leaves," Zoe replied without much enthusiasm.

"Maybe we've got more tuna in the pantry." Lauren's tone matched her cousin's. But it would be a healthy dinner.

They cleaned the space, Annie checking under the tables to make sure there were no lost items, then they trooped down the private hallway into the cottage kitchen.

"What time do we have to be at Zeke's Ridge for our dance lesson?" Lauren asked.

"Seven," Zoe replied.

"Then we'd better grab something."

Lauren fed Annie chicken in gravy, then made their own meal.

While they ate, she told Annie where they were going that evening.

"I hope this teacher is nicer than Simone," Zoe told the feline. "Oops. I mean—"

"I'm sure Annie understands what you meant."

"Brrt!" *Yes!*

Lauren's phone buzzed. She made a disappointed face when she read the text. "Mitch is running late."

"And Chris texted me this afternoon that he'd meet me there. There's a quick meeting after his shift finishes, but it means he won't have time to come here and carpool with us."

"We'd better get ready." Lauren wondered if she'd see more of Mitch after they were married – then banished the thought. *Of course* she would. They'd be sleeping in the same bed for one thing. She just hoped they'd be sleeping in it at the same time.

Lauren said goodbye to Annie, who ambled into the living room and curled up on the sofa, her head resting on the pink velvet cushion Mitch had given her.

"We should be back in a couple of hours," Lauren told her fur baby.

"Brrp," Annie replied a little sleepily.

"She's had a busy day," Lauren whispered to her cousin as they quietly left the house.

"Yeah, she barely had time to snooze in her basket in the café – she was busy talking to her favorite customers a lot!"

They drove to Zeke's Ridge, and pulled up outside the small A-frame dance studio, which was just down the street from Simone's.

"I hope the guys aren't too late," Lauren fretted.

"We'll just have to dance with each other in that case." Zoe winked at her. "I'll lead first, and then you can have a turn."

They got out of the car and headed toward the front door.

"She is so much better than Simone," a slim, blonde girl told her partner as they left the studio. "I can't believe we heard she was hopeless."

Zoe stopped in her tracks, nudged Lauren, then kept walking toward the couple.

"Yeah, she agreed that our paso doble was illegal," her dark-haired partner said in a frustrated voice. "Man, I can't believe Simone tricked us like that."

"Misled more than tricked." The girl frowned at him. "Why would she deliberately deceive us into doing the wrong moves in a competition? It's

not like she was competing herself—"
she grabbed his arm "—was she?"
Her eyes were enormous in her
heart-shaped face.

"I didn't see her at the competition,
but that doesn't mean she didn't
compete earlier." He stopped in his
tracks. "What a dirty thing to do to
students who are paying you to learn
to dance—" he stopped when he
spotted Lauren and Zoe nearby.

"Hi," Lauren said a little awkwardly.

"We couldn't help overhearing,"
Zoe said. She didn't sound
embarrassed. "We saw you at
Simone's studio last week."

"So?" the guy challenged.

"Did you hear that someone killed
her last night?" Lauren asked,
wondering if they were being sensible
questioning him.

"Yes." The girl nodded. "Carol just
told us. She said it was all over town."

"How was your lesson?" Zoe
asked.

"It was amazing." The girl's face lit
up. "She knows so much, and it turns

out that Simone was teaching us the wrong moves."

"I'm sorry to hear that," Lauren said.

"Maybe whoever killed her did me a favor," the guy growled. "Otherwise—" his scowl looked ferocious.

"Dance lessons aren't cheap," the girl put in hastily. "That's why Troy is upset that Simone didn't teach us properly."

"How long have you been dancing?" Zoe asked.

"Nearly six months. Simone said we were ready for our first amateur competition, and we believed her. She *promised* us we'd at least place."

"And instead we came nowhere, Kayla." Her disgruntled partner added.

"I'm sorry," Lauren said.

"Hopefully we'll win the next competition," Troy said.

"Or at least place," Kayla added. "That would be so awesome."

"Do you two want to dance professionally?" Zoe asked curiously.

"That's my dream." Kayla nodded. "Just imagine – entering ball room dancing competitions all over the world!"

"And some of the prize money isn't too shabby," her partner put in.

They headed toward a beat-up black sedan with a yellow sticker on the back.

"I hope Brooke is right about her teacher, and she *is* awesome," Zoe said.

"We'd better go inside."

They entered the studio. Large posters of dancers graced the walls, and gold trophies dotted a bookcase in a corner.

"Hi, I'm Zoe and this is Lauren."

"Hello." A woman turned around and smiled at them.

Lauren drew in a sharp breath.

It was the same person who'd argued with Simone at her dance studio – before she was murdered!

CHAPTER 9

"I'm Carol." In her sixties, she had neat, short blonde-gray hair, her trim figure clad in a long black skirt and matching top.

"It – it's good of you to fit us in like this," Lauren replied.

"Um – yeah." Zoe nodded, catching Lauren's eye.

"Are your partners coming?" Carol asked.

"They're running a little late," Lauren started, "but—"

"I'm here." Mitch strode into the studio and blinked, turning to Lauren with his eyebrow raised.

"Where's Chris?" Zoe looked past him.

"He's on his way."

"Oh, good." Carol said. "Why don't we get started? Who's dancing with whom?"

"Lauren and I are getting married in one and a half weeks." Mitch stood beside her and smiled down at her.

"Lovely. What about you, Zoe? Is Chris your partner?"

"Yes. I'm co-maid of honor and Chris is the best man, so we get to dance together too – plus we're—"

"Sorry." Chris jogged into the room, looking apologetic. "Have you started? The meeting took longer than I thought it would."

"We're just getting to know each other." Carol smiled welcomingly at him. "You must be Chris."

"Yes." He hesitated for a second, then smiled back at her.

"What music are you using for your bridal waltz?" Carol asked Lauren and Mitch.

"*The Blue Danube*," they spoke at once.

"I've got it on my phone in case you don't have it." Zoe dug into her capris.

"I have it on mine." Carol nodded. "Why don't you show me what you've learned so far?"

She turned on the music. Lauren tried to push out the conflicting emotion she felt when she'd recognized Carol. What had she accused Simone of? Badmouthing her, Carol, and saying she was a fraud? Had Simone done that? She'd have to talk about it with the others later.

Mitch held her in his arms and they box-stepped together. She peeked up at his face, glad that he looked relaxed.

"Good, Lauren and Mitch," Carol called out.

Zoe and Chris swept past them, a big smile on her cousin's face.

"Watch your feet a little, Chris," Carol advised. "Otherwise, you're doing well."

When the music stopped, Carol smiled at them.

"I wasn't sure what to expect, but you're all quite good. I don't think you'll have any problems dancing at the wedding."

"That's what I thought." Zoe grinned.

"But after we met the ballroom dancing couple at Simone's—" Lauren began delicately.

"And then she was killed," Zoe added. "We thought maybe we'd better make sure we were as good as we thought we were."

"It *was* sad about Simone." Carol nodded.

"Did you know her?" Chris asked.

"Not really. She was a newcomer to Zeke's Ridge and it sounds like our teaching styles were different," Carol replied diplomatically.

"I'll say," Zoe said.

"This is a bit awkward," Mitch began, "but I'm a detective in Gold Leaf Valley. I came here in my off-duty time to practice with Lauren for our wedding, but I may have to visit you again in an official capacity. I'm now in charge of solving the case."

"That's great!" Lauren smiled at her fiancé.

"The decision was made just before I drove over here," Mitch said.

"Then we can definitely find the killer before the wedding!" Excitement flickered across Zoe's face.

"Do you work for the police as well?" Carol asked.

"No. Lauren and I run the Norwegian Forest Cat Café in Gold Leaf Valley." Zoe beamed. "Along with Annie, Lauren's cat."

"I named the café after her," Lauren added.

"That sounds sweet," Carol replied.

"It is," Zoe told her earnestly. "You should check it out. Annie will even choose a table for you!"

"Really?" Carol asked curiously. "I've heard some students talk about a cat café but—"

"We're happy to give you your first latte on the house," Lauren put in.

"And Lauren makes the best coffee," Zoe told her.

"The cupcakes and pastries are great, too." Chris added.

Mitch nodded.

"Then I'll see if I can drop by when I have some free time." Carol smiled. "Zoe and Chris, do you have special music for your dance? It's usually the first one when the guests are encouraged to take part."

"Um, no." Zoe threw Chris a panicked look.

"We've just been practicing to *The Blue Danube*," Chris added.

"That's the only music Simone used," Lauren said. "She just asked us what sort of dance we wanted to try."

"And since we're pretty traditional, we thought we'd go with a waltz," Mitch ended.

"I see." Carol's lips pursed. "Well, since your wedding is very soon, why don't you choose another waltz, so Zoe and Chris will be comfortable with it?"

"Great idea." Zoe nodded.

"That's fine with me," Chris replied.

"Let's see." Carol picked up her phone. "How about *The Skaters' Waltz*?" Classical strains filled the room.

"I know that tune." Zoe's face lit up.

"Yeah." Chris nodded.

"I think my parents will be pleased," Lauren told Mitch. "The chamber group they hired should be able to play *The Skaters' Waltz*. They said *The Blue Danube* was no problem."

"I think I've got something on my co-maid of honor to do list." Zoe pulled out her phone. "Lauren, you need to give the chamber group your final music list by the end of the week."

"That's right!" Lauren shook her head. "With everything that's happened—"

"Hey, I forgot, too." Mitch wrapped an arm around her.

"We've already started on it." Zoe tapped her screen. "Right here. Your mom wanted some more waltzes, and your dad suggested—"

"Maybe we should talk about this later," Chris suggested, glancing at their teacher.

"It happens all the time," Carol assured them. "Why don't you all try dancing to *The Skaters' Waltz* a few times and see how you do?"

"That would be great." Zoe beamed.

This time, Lauren and Mitch swept past Zoe and Chris. Lauren allowed herself to relax and enjoy the music.

She imagined dancing on the big day, gliding past her guests, and smiled.

After practicing the new waltz four times, Carol turned off the music.

"You're all pretty good," she told them. "I really don't think you need any more lessons before the wedding. Just remember to practice."

"We will," Zoe promised.

They paid Carol, then Zoe wandered over to the other side of the studio, where gold trophies were lined up on a shelf.

"Did you win all these?" Zoe asked curiously.

"Indeed, I did," Carol said. "I had a great partner and we entered a lot of competitions. We won some, and placed in others."

"What happened to him?" Lauren asked.

"He got a great offer in his day job and moved to New York." She sighed. "He encouraged me to go with him, but my life was here. I was already teaching dance and I didn't want to give up this little studio, or my pupils. If I moved to New York, it would mean I'd have to start again with my teaching."

"What did he do?" Zoe wanted to know.

"He had a high up position in human resources," Carol replied.

"Were you two ever—"

"Zoe!" Lauren scolded.

"No, we weren't romantically involved, if that's what you mean." Carol shook her head, looking amused. "But sometimes you find the right dance partner and for whatever reason, you can't dance as well with someone else."

"Is that what happened?" Lauren asked gently.

"Yes. I tried a few other partners, but although we placed at various competitions, it just wasn't the same as it had been with John. So, I decided not to compete anymore, and just dedicated myself to teaching."

"I really enjoyed our lesson today," Chris told her.

"Thank you." Carol smiled. "Please let your friends know about me if they're looking for a dance instructor."

"Brooke recommended us to you, so we'll definitely do the same. Hey!" Zoe nudged Lauren. "If we see Celeste again, we'll tell her how good Carol is."

"Great idea." Lauren nodded.

Carol looked pleased as they said goodbye and headed to their cars.

Lauren drove her and Zoe back, while Mitch and Chris got into their own cars. They'd arranged to meet at the cottage for supper.

"Brrt!" Annie ran to greet Lauren as she opened the front door.

"I missed you, too," Lauren picked her up and held her against her chest.

"We had such a good time at dance class," Zoe told her. "But you'll never guess who the teacher was!"

"Brrt?" *Who?*

"The lady who argued with Simone at her studio when we turned up for our second last lesson," Lauren told her.

"Which turned out to be our last with Simone," Zoe added.

"Brrt!" Annie's green eyes widened as she stared at them.

The guys entered, and they all went into the kitchen. Annie sat on Lauren's lap while Mitch got everyone something to drink.

"We need to give the chamber group the final music list," Lauren reminded her cousin.

"I'll do it now." Zoe whipped out her phone and read through the pieces they'd chosen so far, as well as Lauren's parents' suggestions.

"Sounds good," Mitch said.

"Yeah." Chris nodded.

"Lauren?" Zoe waved her phone.

"Yes. I think Mom will be pleased."

"Okay." Zoe tapped on her phone. "All done."

There was a short silence.

"So," Zoe drew in a breath, "are we going to talk about how weird it was to get a lesson from Carol tonight, when we overheard her arguing with Simone before she died?"

"Before someone killed her," Mitch put in.

"Yeah," Chris said.

"I think she's a better teacher than Simone," Lauren said. "And that ballroom dancing couple thought so, too."

"That's right." Zoe snapped her fingers. "When we arrived there, we met them coming out of the studio and the girl called Kayla was raving about Carol, and even her partner seemed a bit impressed. Then Kayla said maybe Simone competed in the same competition they did, and that's why she taught them the illegal dance moves!"

"I'll have to interview them as well," Mitch said. "And check if Simone did enter that competition – thanks."

"And don't forget what Celeste at the bridal shop mentioned about Simone when we picked up our outfits," Zoe added. "She hit on other grooms as well."

"Apparently," Lauren put in.

Mitch and Chris exchanged a look.

"So a disgruntled bride could have killed Simone," Chris said thoughtfully.

"I'll definitely check into that," Mitch said.

"I'm glad you got the case after all." Lauren smiled at him.

"Brrt!"

"What did Detective Castern do when he got demoted?" Zoe giggled. "Did steam come out of his ears?"

"Nearly." Mitch's eyes crinkled at the corners.

"What reason did your boss give for taking him off the case?" Chris asked.

"I don't know." Mitch shrugged. "It was done privately in my boss's office. Castern stormed out, then I was called in and told to work the case and to do it quickly before my wedding." He smiled. "I wasn't going to argue with that."

He turned to Lauren, sitting next to him. "It probably means I'll even see you less than I am now – at least until we're married. But it will be worth it if we can have our big day and then the honeymoon without Simone's murder hanging over our heads."

"Yes, it *will* be worth it." Lauren leaned into him.

"Brrt," Annie agreed.

Chris offered to cook some pasta for them, and Zoe found a jar of tomato and mushroom sauce in the pantry.

"I think we'll need to get a lot of groceries this week," Lauren told her cousin. They usually went to the supermarket on Mondays, their day off, but lately Lauren hadn't been as organized as usual, and they hadn't bought much at the grocery store besides Mrs. Finch's coffee pods on Monday.

The guys cleaned up, then went home. Sometimes Mitch spent the night, and Zoe stayed at Chris's house, but lately everyone had been too busy with wedding preparations and work to think about staying overnight.

Lauren said goodnight to Zoe, then she and Annie curled up together in her bedroom. Stroking the silver-gray tabby's velvety soft fur, she fell asleep before she could think about anything else.

CHAPTER 10

"Where's my cutie pie?" The next day, their friend Martha barreled into the café, pushing her rolling walker. Her fuchsia sweat pants and matching sweater complimented her curly gray hair.

"Brrt!" Annie trotted to greet her, jumping onto the black vinyl padded seat.

"Where are we sitting today?"

"Brrt!" *Over here!* Annie directed her to a large table near the counter, with a series of brrps and brrts.

"Hi, Martha." Lauren headed over.

"What can we get you?" Zoe zipped past Lauren, a big smile on her face.

"I'd love my marshmallow latte." Martha grinned. "And what sort of cupcakes do you have today?"

"Triple chocolate ganache, Norwegian apple, and red velvet," Lauren replied.

"Can I have all three?" Martha laughed at her joke. "It's too hard to decide – but I think I'll have the red velvet."

"Coming right up."

"Nearly everyone has tried your marshmallow latte," Zoe told her. "I have it most of the time now."

"I'm glad you girls are raking in the profits." Martha winked at them.

"I'm charging thirty cents extra for the marshmallows," Lauren confided.

"It's boosted our bottom line a little," Zoe added.

They headed back to the counter to start the order. Annie stayed at the table, talking to Martha in a series of brrts and brrps.

"Hey, we can ask Martha if she knew Simone." Zoe snapped her fingers.

"Good idea." Lauren concentrated on steaming the milk, then adding a spoonful of pink and white mini marshmallows, stirring the concoction carefully.

Zoe plated the cupcake. Lauren knew from extensive taste testing that the red cake crumb, flavored with cocoa and a hint of vanilla, melted in the mouth, while the cream cheese frosting gave it a deliciously tangy flavor.

Zoe looked sideways at Lauren. "Are you thinking up a new creation before the wedding?"

"No," she replied regretfully. "With everything else I have to do, plus bake all the vanilla cupcakes for the tower and decorate them, I've decided it will be too stressful." She'd reached that decision in the middle of last night, when she'd woken from a dream that had her running all over the café kitchen juggling identical cupcakes iced with the words: *Is this new?*

"I hear you." Zoe nodded, then looked concerned. "Let me know if I can help in any way. I could make the decorations with you."

"Thanks, but I think I can manage on my own." Lauren gave her a warm smile. She knew her cousin meant well, but her previous attempts with fondant had been a little misshapen.

"I know I'm not as good as you in the kitchen," Zoe said ruefully. "Just let me know if you need me to do anything else." She tapped her jeans' pocket. "I double-checked last night and I'm up to date with my co-maid of honor to do list."

"That's great." She reached out and touched her cousin's arm. "Thank you."

They brought Martha's order over to her.

"I've been looking forward to my treat all morning." Martha picked up the mug and took a sip of the frothy marshmallow infused coffee. "Mmm. I do love my marshmallows."

Since the café was relatively quiet, they joined her.

"Did you hear about our dance instructor?" Zoe began.

"Yep." Martha nodded.

"Did you know her?" Lauren asked.

"Nope." Martha shook her head. "But the news is buzzing around the senior center. Apparently, some of the members had lessons with her two months ago – an old married couple had a golden wedding anniversary, and wanted to brush up on their dancing."

"And?" Zoe prompted.

"The wife didn't like her but the husband did." Martha chuckled. "And I can guess why after the wife described Simone's outfit."

Lauren's mind flashed back to their instructor's gauzy tops and flowing skirts showing off her toned figure.

"What are you two going to do about dance lessons now? Or had you finished them before – you know."

"We had a lesson with Brooke's teacher, Carol," Lauren replied.

"She was great." Zoe glanced sideways at Lauren, and as if by silent agreement, they didn't mention the argument they'd overheard Carol have with Simone, when she accused the cougar of calling her a fraud.

"Are you having more lessons with her?" Martha asked.

"She said we didn't need any more," Lauren answered.

"Huh. An honest dance teacher. That makes a change from the little I've heard about Simone."

"What do you mean?" Lauren's eyes widened.

"Brrt?"

"The golden wedding anniversary wife told me that Simone said they were very rusty, and would need a ton of lessons if they didn't want to embarrass themselves on the dance floor. She even wanted them to sign up for a course of twelve, and pay in advance."

Lauren and Zoe looked at each other.

"You two didn't do that, did you?"

"It was a course of eight," Lauren replied.

"And we got all our lessons, apart from the last one."

"And you paid in advance?" Martha guessed.

"We thought maybe that's how dance instructors do things these days," Lauren offered.

"Yeah, and I'd already contacted two other places and they were full,"

Zoe added. "So I thought we'd better sign up with Simone since she had spots available."

"I guess I can't blame you." Martha set down her mug. "Your wedding is next weekend! I've bought you a little gift on your registry list, and bought you a toy, Annie. I got it from the animal shelter, so they'll get a cut of the profits."

"Brrt!" *Thank you.* Annie stared at Martha with wide green eyes, as if expecting the present to materialize any second.

"I haven't got it on me now, cutie pie. I thought I'd give it to you on the big day." She winked at Annie.

"That's very kind of you, Martha." Lauren smiled at their friend.

"Definitely." Zoe nodded, her brunette pixie bangs bouncing against her forehead.

More customers entered, so they excused themselves and headed to the counter. Annie took up her hostess duties, greeting and seating each newcomer, then returned to Martha.

Just before the lunch rush, Mitch strode in.

"I can only stay a minute." He leaned over the counter and kissed her swiftly.

"Latte?" she asked, her heart fluttering a little. It was good to see him, even if it was for just a moment.

"Please." He nodded. "The boss has told Castern to interview the bridal shop manager about what she heard from the dissatisfied brides who took dance lessons with Simone."

"Do you know when Simone was killed?" Zoe jumped into the conversation as Lauren ground the beans and steamed the milk, the espresso machine making a growling noise.

"It looks like it was before seven p.m. – just before we got there."

"What about witnesses?" Zoe pressed.

"There weren't any that we could find." Mitch's lips firmed.

Lauren handed him the cardboard cup, as well as a red velvet.

"Thanks." His dark brown eyes crinkled at the corners. "I'd suggest dinner tonight, but I might be working late."

"I understand." She nodded.

"Carol said we had to practice," Zoe reminded them.

"Will you have time to come over on the weekend?" Lauren glanced at him.

"Good idea." Zoe tapped her cheek. "I'll see if Chris can make it too, and we can have a waltzing party." She giggled.

"I should be able to make it sometime." Leaning over the counter, Mitch murmured to her, "I miss you."

"I miss you, too."

He gave her a rueful smile, then his phone buzzed. Glancing at it, he sighed. "I've got to go."

"We now have our first sleuthing task," Zoe announced once Mitch departed.

"Oh?"

"We have to talk to Celeste at the bridal shop."

"We do?"

"Yes." Zoe furrowed her brow. "We can't leave it to Detective Castern to bungle his interview with her."

"But hasn't she already told us the gossip about Simone?" Lauren queried. "What else could she tell us about her?"

"She might have an idea who killed her. What if one of the brides who complained to her about Simone was really steamed? Steamed enough to kill?"

"You do have a point," Lauren said slowly, her heart sinking. "But when are we going to fit this in? Remember, I have to bake a ton of cupcakes next week for the wedding, and decorate them."

"That's next week." Zoe airily waved a hand in the air. "The only thing we've got on for the rest of the week is craft club tomorrow night and waltzing practice on the weekend. *And,* the bridal shop is open late tonight." Her brown eyes sparkled.

"How convenient," Lauren said dryly.

"It is, isn't it?" Zoe ignored her cousin's tone. "So, I say we go there after we close at five, and grill Celeste!"

CHAPTER 11

After closing the café right on the dot of five, cleaning, and giving Annie her dinner at the cottage, Lauren sank onto a kitchen chair.

"Are you sure we need to interview Celeste at the bridal shop?" she asked.

"Yes," Zoe replied. "And we'd better skedaddle. She closes at seven-thirty."

Lauren checked her watch. Just before six.

"Okay." She sighed. "We'll have to grab dinner on the way home."

"That's what I was thinking." Zoe grinned. "We can stop at a fast-food joint."

Lauren hoped it was one that included salad on their menu. She definitely wanted to fit into her gown.

Explaining to Annie what they were up to, she dropped a kiss on the feline's forehead.

"We won't be long," Zoe assured her.

"We can all watch TV when we get back," Lauren promised.

"Brrt." *Good.*

Annie ambled toward the living room.

"Let's go." Zoe zipped out of the kitchen.

Lauren followed, hoping the bridal shop manager wouldn't be offended by their – Zoe's – questioning.

Lauren observed the speed limit on the highway, and about an hour later, they arrived in Sacramento. She found a parking spot a few doors down from the shop.

"Awesome!" Zoe jumped out of the car. "Come on!"

Lauren wondered if they were doing the right thing – had Detective Castern even interviewed Celeste yet? Had Zoe thought of that? She was just about to ask her cousin, when she saw her open the door, the bell tinkling above her head.

With an inward sigh, Lauren followed.

"Zoe. Lauren." Celeste looked up from the register, a quizzical smile on her face. "Is everything okay with your outfits?"

"Yes," Lauren hastened to assure her. "I love my gown."

"And I love my gorgeous co-maid of honor outfit," Zoe added. "We're here about Simone. Has a Detective Castern been to see you?"

"No." Celeste wrinkled her brow. "No one from law enforcement has visited me today. Why? Is something wrong?"

"We want to make sure Simone's murder is solved before Lauren's wedding," Zoe explained.

Lauren flushed. "And since you mentioned you'd heard about Simone's behavior," she began delicately, "we thought—"

"We'd ask you a little more about it," Zoe finished. "Because Detective Castern isn't very—"

"Zoe," Lauren warned.

"Mmm – you might be right." Zoe made a moue. "Anyway, what we wanted to know was, who told you about Simone trying to steal people's boyfriends or grooms away from them? Maybe they had a motive to kill her, because Simone actually did it!"

"Did what?" Celeste looked a little puzzled.

"Stole their significant other," Zoe explained. "Maybe her come hither charm actually worked on one of the grooms, and the bride-to-be was furious and BAM! She killed Simone for revenge."

Celeste looked like she was stifling a smile.

"Well, I can't think of anyone offhand," she began.

"When did you first hear rumors about Simone?" Lauren prompted.

"Oh, let me see, a few months ago." She nodded. "Yes, that's right. One of my brides came into the shop, crying, because she said Simone had flirted with her fiancé, and he'd flirted back. I tried to calm her down and said at least it was only flirting, and he did it right in front of her, although in hindsight maybe that wasn't the wisest thing to say. But surely it's better for a man to be silly in plain sight of his bride than going behind her back?"

"I see your point. Sort of." Zoe nodded. "What about other brides? Did they have the same problem with Simone?"

"Some of them," Celeste replied. "It seems that Simone has taught all over California and has ruffled a few brides along the way. Some of my clients have come to see me after the wedding and told me they were complimented a lot on their dress." She smiled. "But a few of them did say they'd felt a bit let down in their lessons with her. It turns out they weren't quite as good on the dance floor as they thought they would be, and some of the other guests turned out to be better dancers than they were."

Lauren and Zoe exchanged a slightly panicked look.

"We'd better make sure we practice on the weekend," Lauren said.

"Uh-huh."

They chatted to Celeste for a few more minutes, but didn't glean any more interesting tidbits about Simone.

"Oh, by the way," Zoe said when they were about to depart, "please tell your brides that Carol at Zeke's Ridge is an amazing dance teacher."

"She is." Lauren nodded.

"Will do," Celeste replied with a smile. "Thanks for the recommendation."

On the way home, they stopped at a fast-food place for a quick dinner in the car. Zoe enjoyed a huge burger and fries, while Lauren nibbled on a meat patty wrapped in lettuce and an extra helping of salad. Zoe encouraged her to pinch some of her fries.

"Now we get to relax at home with Annie," Zoe said in satisfaction, balling up the food wrappers and placing them in a paper bag Lauren specifically kept for such a purpose.

"I'll have to tell Mitch we just spoke to the bridal shop manager," she reminded Zoe.

"You could do that tomorrow."

"I think I'll do it when we get home."

Lauren drove them home. Annie greeted them, leading them into the living room.

"Brrt." She patted the TV remote sitting on the coffee table.

"You want to watch something now?" Lauren pushed the button and the screen came to life.

"Brrt!" Annie jumped onto the pink sofa and stared at the screen.

"No way!" Zoe sucked in a breath. "The princess movie has a sequel?"

"Brrt!" *Yes!*

Lauren sank onto the sofa, and Annie nestled into her lap. She'd call Mitch first thing tomorrow morning and inform him about their sleuthing. Right now, she was going to enjoy watching another movie about the princess who discovered her whole life was a lie, apart from being a princess.

CHAPTER 12

"That sequel was amazing last night." Zoe slathered butter onto whole-wheat toast the next morning.

"It was," Lauren agreed.

"Brrt!"

Zoe snapped her fingers. "We'd better call Father Mike and let him know about it. Mrs. Snuggle liked watching the original movie."

"That's true." The fluffy white Persian had watched it a few times when they'd looked after her earlier that year.

Zoe munched her toast, then called Father Mike, who hadn't known about the second princess movie.

"He's going to put it on for Mrs. Snuggle tonight." She giggled. "Said it was going to be a surprise for her."

"How did you know about it, Annie?" Lauren thought back to the previous evening, when Annie had asked them to turn on the television.

"Cat magic." Zoe winked at Annie.

"Brrt!"

After breakfast, they trooped through the private hallway to the café. Annie ambled around the space, nosing into each corner, but not finding anything interesting.

Zoe unstacked the chairs, while Lauren baked the cupcakes, greeting Ed, who was already busy rolling out his light and flaky Danish pastry.

"Not long 'til the wedding now," he greeted her.

"No," she replied. "Are you still bringing Rebecca as your plus one?"

He'd met the fellow volunteer at the local animal shelter and they'd started dating.

"Yep." His white teeth flashed briefly. "She's looking forward to it."

"Great." She returned his smile.

After the cupcakes came out of the oven, she left them to cool and joined Annie and Zoe in the café.

"Oh, I have to call Mitch." She fished out her phone from her capris' pocket. She'd completely forgotten she'd meant to tell him about visiting the bridal shop manager last night.

He answered, and she quickly told him about their sleuthing last night.

"I should have guessed," he said wryly. "I heard Castern muttering this morning about having to drive over there today before he stomped out of the office."

Lauren reminded him it was craft club tonight, then asked if he could make it to the cottage the following evening.

"If Chris is available as well, we can all practice our waltzing."

"Good idea." His voice was warm. "I'll text him about it."

They talked for another minute before they said goodbye.

"Well?" Zoe looked up from the latte she was making for herself. "What did Mitch say?"

Lauren gave her the gist of the conversation.

Zoe's phone buzzed and she dug it out of her pocket. And smiled. "Chris can make it to our waltzing party."

"Great."

"And he and Mitch will fix dinner for us."

"Even better."

"Definitely."

***

Later that morning, Carol, the dance teacher from Zeke's Ridge, popped in.

"Hi," Lauren greeted her, remembering her offer of a free latte.

"Hi, Lauren." She wore tan slacks and a cream sweater.

Annie was in her pink cat basket. She shook herself and walked over to the newcomer.

"Brrt?" She reached up a paw to pat the dangling ribbon Carol held between her fingertips.

"I found this outside. It's such a pretty shade of blue with these white daisies on it."

"It *is* cute," Zoe agreed, taking it from her. She held it up so Lauren could see.

"Maybe it slipped off someone's hair," she mused. Hadn't Carol called it blue? To her, it definitely looked purple.

"We'll put it in our drawer and keep it safe," Zoe declared.

Carol handed over the ribbon and Zoe hurried behind the counter and slid it into the drawer.

"Thank you." Carol smiled.

"Annie will show you to a table," Lauren advised her.

"Brrt!" Annie led the dance instructor to a small table in the middle of the room.

"This will be the perfect time to ask her about her confrontation with Simone," muttered Zoe.

"Do you really think so?"

"Of course. I'll go over and take her order while you get started on her complimentary latte."

"Yes, boss," Lauren murmured under her breath, pressing the button on the coffee grinder. A loud growling ensued. Usually, it was Zoe who called Lauren "boss".

She watched Zoe talk to Carol. Annie joined them, sitting opposite Carol at the table, her green eyes alert.

"She's asked for an apricot Danish." Zoe zipped back to the counter and plated the flaky pastry.

"The latte's just about ready." Lauren focused on creating a peacock on top of the micro foam.

"That will really blow her away." Zoe admired the latte art.

They headed over to the table with the order.

"Thank you." Carol peered at the top of her foam. "Goodness, this looks very professional."

"Thank," Lauren replied.

"That's because we *are* professionals," Zoe replied. "Well, Lauren is."

Zoe had always been her biggest cheerleader. She hoped she was Zoe's.

"Are there any leads on Simone's murder?" Carol took a sip. "Mmm. You were right when you said you were professionals. This is the best coffee I've had anywhere lately."

"Thank you." Lauren smiled. It always made her feel good when her coffee and cupcakes were praised.

"No leads as far as we know," Zoe replied.

"Isn't your fiancé a police detective, Lauren?" Carol wrinkled her brow. "I was sure you told me that at your dance lesson."

"He is," she replied. "But—"

"Mitch is working the case right now." Zoe leaned over the table. "Has he come to see you yet?"

"No."

"We couldn't help overhearing when we arrived at Simone's studio for a lesson," Zoe continued, "you accused Simone of calling you a fraud."

"Brrt?" Annie looked at Carol inquiringly, her ears pricked.

"Oh, that." Carol gave a little laugh. "It seems a bit petty, now that Simone is dead. But, if you really want to know …?" She shrugged.

"Yes." Zoe's brown eyes gleamed with curiosity. "We do."

"Well, I found out, quite by accident, that Simone had been going around town – and goodness knows where else – telling people that I was a fraud, and I hadn't won all my ballroom dancing trophies."

"Really?" Lauren blinked.

"Yes." Carol nodded. "I even lost some new students over it, who didn't know me well enough to realize that I'm a good teacher, and that all my trophies are the real deal."

"I'm sorry to hear that," Lauren said. And she was.

"If it helps, we recommended you to Celeste, the bridal shop manager, in Sacramento yesterday. The bridal boutique that's really popular. Our friend Brooke got her dress there and recommended it to us, and we got our outfits there."

"Oh, yes, I've heard of that shop," Carol replied. "Some of my students have raved about their gown from there. Well, thank you." She smiled. "I do appreciate that."

"We really enjoyed our lesson with you as well," Lauren said.

"Yeah, it was great. And we're going to practice our waltzing tomorrow night with the guys."

"I'm glad to hear that." Carol took another sip of her latte.

"Did you hear or see anything around the time of the murder?" Zoe continued. "Your studio is just down the street from Simone's."

"I'm afraid not." Carol picked up a fork. "I was watching television at the time. I'd had a busy day teaching, and decided to take a break before my evening lesson. I have a TV in the back room." She popped a morsel into her mouth. "This is delicious."

"I'll tell Ed," Lauren replied. "He makes the pastries."

"And Lauren creates all the cupcakes."

"Brrt!"

"But surely there were people closer to Simone's studio?" Carol asked. "At the time of the – you know. Maybe they saw or heard something?"

"Mitch is checking that out," Zoe replied.

"I hope he finds out who did it." Carol nodded.

They left her to enjoy her treats and headed back to the counter. Annie returned to her basket.

The lunch rush arrived, keeping all three of them hopping.

"Phew!" Zoe theatrically mopped her brow around two-thirty. They'd each managed to grab a bite during brief lulls, and were now recovering from the steady stream of customers.

"I feel like one of Martha's marshmallow lattes." Lauren looked wistfully at the jar of marshmallows next to the espresso machine. "But I don't think I can be bothered to get up." She sat on a stool behind the counter, rotating her sneaker-clad feet.

"I hear you." Zoe nodded. "But I'm desperate for one too, so I'll make them."

"Thanks." Lauren smiled at her gratefully.

They sipped the fawn, pink, and white frothy beverage in appreciation.

"Even Annie looks tuckered out," Zoe observed.

The feline was curled up in a ball, sleeping peacefully.

A few customers entered in the next hour, and then the glass and oak entrance door opened to reveal two of their friends – tall, athletic Claire, and her little daughter Molly.

"Annie!" Molly beamed as she stood at the *Please Wait to be Seated* sign, her blonde curls tousled.

"How was big school?" Zoe asked.

"Brrt?" Annie trotted up to greet the little girl.

"I love it!" Molly sighed happily. She looked up at Claire. "Don't I, Mommy?"

"You certainly do." Claire smiled. Dressed in yoga pants and an apricot sweater, she held Molly's hand. "Oh, that's what I needed to ask all of you. Molly lost—"

"Brrt!" Annie scampered over to the counter and looked up at Lauren.

"It's not a ribbon with white daisies?" Lauren opened the drawer and held out the hair decoration.

"Yes!" Molly clapped her hands together in delight. "That's mine!"

"Did Annie find it?" Claire asked. "Molly loves that purple ribbon."

Lauren rounded the counter and handed the ribbon to Molly.

"Not this time," Zoe answered. "A customer found it this morning."

"It must have slipped off her hair on the way to school," Claire explained. "I would have dropped in for a latte afterward, but it was too early."

"But Annie knew it was yours, didn't you?" Lauren bent down to her fur baby.

"Brrt!" *Yes, I did!*

"Cino?" Molly looked hopefully at Lauren and Zoe.

"Of course," Lauren replied with a smile, "as long as it's okay with your mom."

"Yes," Claire replied. "She certainly enjoys it." She stroked her daughter's hair. "And I'll have a large latte and one of your cupcakes." She glanced at the glass case. "Do you have any left?"

"We have Norwegian apple, and super vanilla."

Claire chose the fruit-based cupcake.

Annie led the duo over to a large table near the counter and hopped up in a chair next to Molly's. The little girl gently petted the silver-gray tabby with "fairy pats".

Lauren made the latte, and the babycino, which consisted of milk froth, pink and white marshmallows, and a dusting of chocolate powder, served in an espresso sized cup.

Zoe plated the cupcake, and waited until the beverages were ready. They took the order over to them.

"How's Kitty?" Zoe asked Molly.

"Brrt?" Annie looked at the little girl.

"Love her," Molly sighed. She beamed at the feline. "And you, Annie."

"Brrt." *Thank you.*

Molly had fallen in love with the little scrap who looked similar to Annie when the cafe had hosted the kitten adoption day a while ago, and had named her Kitty.

"Here are the latest photos." Claire pulled out her phone and showed them images of Molly and Kitty playing together, happy expressions on both their faces.

"They look so cute together." Lauren smiled.

"They even sleep together," Claire told them.

"Yeah." Molly giggled, then looked from Annie to Lauren, then Zoe. "I'm going to be at the wedding!"

"Yes, you are," Claire said. "We all are. Thank you again for inviting us. Molly can't wait."

"Annie and I have been practicing walking down the aisle," Zoe told the little girl, "Because we're co-maids of honor."

"Ooh!"

"And we're going to wear flowers in our hair." Zoe touched her dark locks.

"Molly wear flowers?" She looked hopefully at her mom.

"You have daisies on your ribbon." Claire patted her pocket. "I should wash it before she wears it again."

"Wear flowers at wedding? Lauren will be a pwincess! I want to be a pwincess!"

"Brrt!"

"I think Annie does as well." Zoe giggled.

"She still loves watching cartoons about princesses," Claire explained.

Lauren glanced at Zoe, thinking about the movie Annie loved watching – as well as Mrs. Snuggle.

"We should tell Claire." Zoe nodded.

They told her about the princess movie the cats loved watching – and so did they.

"I don't know if it will be too old for Molly, though." Lauren crinkled her brow.

"I haven't heard about that movie, but I'll definitely check it out and see if it's suitable for her," Claire replied. "She might have to wait a few years, though."

"For what?" Molly asked curiously. While her mother had been busy chatting to Lauren and Zoe, she'd sneaked a few bites of the Norwegian apple cupcake, frosting smeared around her lips.

She picked up the tiny cup and drank the frothy cino, giving herself a pink, white, and chocolate moustache as well.

Smacking her lips, she announced, "Yum!"

Claire glanced at her daughter and smiled, before whipping out a tissue and gently wiping Molly's face.

Looking down at the half-eaten cupcake on her plate, Claire exclaimed in a teasing tone, "Did you leave any for me?"

"Yummy, Mommy."

"The girls were telling me about a movie you might enjoy," Claire added, picking up her fork and slicing into the remains of the cupcake, "but it might be a little old for you at the moment."

Molly pouted, then resumed "fairy patting" Annie, who closed her eyes in appreciation.

Lauren and Zoe chatted with them for a few more minutes, Molly's sunny nature bouncing back quickly.

A few more customers arrived, so Lauren and Zoe said goodbye and headed to the counter.

Soon, it was five o'clock, and time to close up.

"Craft club tonight," Zoe announced. "I can't wait to tell Mrs. Finch about our sleuthing efforts!

CHAPTER 13

"Are you okay, Mrs. Finch?" Lauren asked that evening. "You haven't been to the café much this week." They'd arrived at their friend's house and were now settled in the living room.

"I'm fine, Lauren," the senior answered. "Just a little tired."

"Can we get you anything?" Zoe asked.

"A latte a bit later would be lovely, dear," she replied. "Now, why don't you tell me what you've been up to this week? Lauren, did you bring your knitting with you?"

"Yes." Lauren dug it out of her bag and looked at the red and purple scarf a little dubiously. The large ball of yarn was still pretty big. "I hope I'll finish this for your Christmas present, Zoe. Maybe I should try to get some done on my honeymoon."

"I don't think Mitch would approve." Her cousin giggled.

"Perhaps not."

"You'll be too busy sightseeing, going to the beach, and whatever else honeymooners do in Hawaii." Zoe winked at her.

"I do hope you'll have a lovely time, Lauren dear." Mrs. Finch nodded.

"I'm sure I – we – will." Lauren wrapped the wool around her fingers and click-clacked a few stitches.

"Now tell me, how is Mitch getting along with this investigation? I hope he can find out who the killer is – we don't want anything to ruin your big day."

"No, we don't," Zoe said seriously.

They'd told their friend when they'd arrived that Mitch had been put in charge of the case.

They updated her on what they knew, including their visit to the bridal shop, and their waltzing lesson with Carol.

"She's such a good teacher," Zoe enthused. "And she charged us less than Simone did for one lesson."

"And Simone said we'd get a small discount if we prepaid for eight lessons in advance," Lauren added a little indignantly.

"So either Simone was more expensive than we thought, or she ripped us off by not giving us a discount." Zoe's mouth pursed.

"Have you heard of Carol, Mrs. Finch?" Lauren asked.

"Yes, I believe I have." She nodded. Annie jumped down from her place on the sofa next to Lauren, trotted over to their friend, and hopped up on the arm of Mrs. Finch's chair.

"Brrp."

Mrs. Finch smiled and stroked the silver-gray tabby with a wobbly hand.

"People used to say Carol was a marvelous dancer. So was her partner. That's when they competed. But I'm afraid I don't get out and about as much as I used to, so I haven't heard much lately. But people did say she was a good dance instructor as well."

"So why did Simone badmouth Carol?" Zoe tapped her cheek.

"That's what Carol told us today." She glanced at Lauren.

"That's right." She nodded. "Maybe Simone wasn't as good a teacher as she thought she was? Remember, she only had us practicing to one waltz tune during our lessons, and didn't ask what music you and Chris wanted to try for the first dance for everyone."

"That's right! I thought Carol looked a little – surprised – when we told her that."

"Have you decided on a piece of music, Zoe?" Mrs. Finch asked.

"*The Skaters' Waltz*. The four of us are practicing tomorrow night."

"Brrp," Annie agreed.

"Annie, you can be the judge and tell us if Chris and I are the best, or if Lauren and Mitch are." Zoe giggled.

"Brrt!" *Good idea!* Annie's green eyes sparkled.

The three of them chuckled, Annie joining in with a happy brrp.

They talked about the upcoming bachelorette party next week. Instead of holding it the night before the wedding, they'd decided to have it on the Thursday night instead. Mrs. Finch was hosting it.

"It won't be too much work for you?" Lauren asked in concern.

"Of course not," Mrs. Finch assured her. "You girls are bringing everything, anyway. Remind me who's coming?"

"Brrt!" *Yes!*

"Claire, Brooke, Martha, Ms. Tobin," Zoe rattled off the names.

"It sounds lovely," Mrs. Finch replied. "And what about Mitch, Lauren? Is he doing anything?"

"He's getting together with Chris and a few other friends as far as I know," Lauren replied.

"They're having it on the same night we are. Hey!" Zoe nudged Lauren. "Wouldn't it be funny if they ended up crashing our party?"

"They're more than welcome," Mrs. Finch said seriously.

After chatting for a bit longer, they made their friend a latte using her capsule machine, then said goodbye to her.

"We'll drop by on Sunday to say hello," Lauren promised.

"That would be lovely." Mrs. Finch smiled.

"We've got a busy week ahead," Zoe told them as they drove home, the car's headlights lighting the way. "Waltzing practice, finding the killer, and last-minute wedding prep."

"Brrt!"

CHAPTER 14

Saturday afternoon, Lauren relaxed on the sofa with Annie nestled beside her. They'd opened the café as usual that morning, and sold out in record time. She didn't know where their customers were going to get their cupcake fix next weekend!

She and Zoe had agreed to close the café while Lauren was on her honeymoon, as she was worried it would be too stressful for Zoe to handle the customers on her own, even with Annie as her assistant, and the occasional help from Ed when he wasn't busy baking his pastries. Sometimes it was amazing the three of them coped during a busy lunch rush.

She looked at the travel brochure on her lap.

"This is where Mitch and I will be." She pointed to a white sandy beach, turquoise waters, and a beautiful sky. "Hawaii."

"Brrt?" Annie patted the photo of the beach.

"And Zoe will be looking after you here."

"Brrp." Annie's lower lip protruded for a moment, as if she were pouting.

"It will only be for a week," she assured her fur baby. "When Mitch and I come back, he'll be living here with us, and Zoe will be staying in his apartment. But she'll still be working with us in the café, and coming over all the time for dinner."

She'd told Annie about the impending changes in their lives a few times, hoping she would understand.

"Brrp," her fur baby replied thoughtfully. Her pout had disappeared.

Lauren nearly dozed off as she slowly stroked Annie, the silver-gray fur like velvet under her fingertips.

"Ready to waltz?" Zoe's voice woke her with a start.

"What?" Lauren blinked, and sat upright.

"I won't tell Mitch I caught you napping." Zoe giggled.

"Can you blame me?" Lauren yawned behind her hand. "With everything that's been happening—"

"And you still have to bake all those cupcakes for next weekend. Luckily, we're – you're – only having fifty-four guests. How many are you going to make?"

"I hadn't decided yet," Lauren replied guiltily. "At least two per person, but I've been thinking I should make it three."

"That would be one-hundred-and-sixty-two," Zoe said after a moment. "Which is—"

"Thirteen and a half dozen. I should round it up to fourteen." Since her cupcake pans held twelve, and not a baker's dozen of thirteen, that would be a total of one-hundred-and-sixty-eight cupcakes.

"I'll have to take a proper inventory tomorrow at the café, and make sure I have enough ingredients for them, as well as the normal baking during the week." Lauren flopped back against the pink sofa cushions.

"I'll put that on my wedding to-do list." Zoe dug out her phone from her jeans' pocket. "I thought we could move some of the furniture back for our waltzing." She glanced at the screen. "The guys will be coming in a couple of hours."

"Already?" Lauren checked her watch. "Why didn't you tell me?" She began to rise.

"I didn't want to interrupt you and Annie." Zoe smiled at them. "You were having a moment with looking at the honeymoon brochure, and then when I popped in a bit later, you looked so peaceful snuggled with her, I thought I should let you rest for a bit."

"Thanks." Lauren was touched by her cousin's thoughtfulness.

She took a quick shower, then stood in front of her closet, wondering what to wear. Sometimes she still couldn't believe she was marrying Mitch in one week – by this time next Saturday, he would be her husband!

Finally deciding on her plum wrap dress, which was one of Mitch's favorites, she slipped on her kitten heels.

"Brrt?" Annie wandered into the bedroom and jumped onto the bed.

"I'm getting ready for waltzing practice," she told her, brushing her hair. Brooke had trimmed it a couple of weeks ago, in her usual shoulder length style, so hopefully it would look just right for the wedding. The hair stylist had suggested some blonde highlights, but Lauren preferred to keep the natural hints of gold that lightened her brown hair.

Surveying herself in the mirror, she thought she'd lost a couple of pounds. Maybe all those salads had paid off, after all. But she still had the curves she'd grown up with, and thought she always would.

When the guys arrived, they suggested they eat first and practice later.

"Otherwise, it might be too late for dinner," Chris said.

"Sounds good to me." Zoe grinned.

Mitch had brought sirloin steaks with him – one of his favorite meals.

"I've got some for Annie as well." He crouched down and held the bag out to the feline. "Would you like it now?'

"Brrt!" *Yes, please!*

Lauren offered to cut up the steak, but Mitch waved her away. "I'm happy to do it."

Lauren sat at the kitchen table, watching her fiancé in her kitchen. Although, she reminded herself, after the wedding it would be *their* kitchen.

Zoe joined her, flopping onto the pine chair. "I hope you don't have salad in that bag," she warned Chris.

He turned around, frowning. "I do, actually."

"Kidding. It's just that Lauren and I have eaten a lot of green stuff this week." Zoe smiled at him.

"Then you'll like my steaks." Mitch placed the meat in the pan, causing a hissing noise.

"Definitely," Zoe agreed.

"Brrt!" Annie finished her meal, her little pink tongue lapping up any left-over juices, then jumped on the chair next to Lauren.

"How's the case going?" she asked.

"Castern said he interviewed Celeste, the bridal shop manager, but said she didn't have any interesting information to give him."

"And you believed him?" Zoe frowned.

"I went over his report thoroughly, but he didn't come up with anything new. In fact, you and Lauren got more gossip from the manager than he did."

"Just call me Detective Zoe." Her cousin grinned.

"Did Simone enter the same ballroom dancing competition Kayla and her partner did?" Lauren asked.

"Not that I could find out." Mitch flipped the steaks.

"So why would she teach them illegal dance moves if she's not competing against them?" Zoe tapped her cheek.

"Because she's not very good?" Chris rinsed some cherry tomatoes and placed them in the salad bowl.

"Yeah, maybe that's why she has to use her womanly wiles on the men." Zoe nodded.

"Not that it worked on us." Mitch turned around and looked directly at Lauren, as if to reassure her.

"I know," she said softly. And she did.

"Yeah." Zoe gave Chris a confident nod.

"Have you interviewed Kayla and her partner Troy?" Chris asked.

"Not yet." Mitch frowned. "I went to see them, but they'd finished work early. Troy works in a warehouse, and Kayla has a job in a boutique in Sacramento."

"Maybe they were at Carol's studio, having another lesson," Lauren suggested.

"I checked that out. She said they were booked for next week."

"Maybe they took off for a couple of days to enjoy the weekend," Zoe offered. "And to discuss their plans to dominate the ballroom dancing world."

"They did seem pretty serious about it," Lauren added.

"What about Carol's alibi for the time of Simone's murder?" Chris asked.

"She was watching TV," Zoe replied.

Both guys turned to look at her.

"How do you know that?" Mitch asked.

"I asked her yesterday when she came into the café."

"I offered her a latte on the house on her first visit," Lauren explained.

Annie was listening to the conversation with her gray ears pricked.

"I spoke to her yesterday afternoon and you're right, she said she was watching television at the time, in the back room of her dance studio. Carol described the show to me, and I checked the episode, and she was correct about the details, but …"

"What?" Lauren asked.

"The episode was a re-run, so she could have seen it at an earlier time."

"But Carol is so nice," Zoe stated. "I loved our lesson with her."

"I did too," Lauren agreed.

"Just because no one can corroborate her alibi doesn't mean she's guilty," Mitch said. "But it does mean I have to dig deeper to find out who had a problem with Simone."

"A problem big enough to kill for," Chris agreed.

"I checked with the company who delivered Simone's special dance shoes – the ones with the purple swirls – and they confirmed Simone accepted the delivery – she had to sign digitally for it – and we saw her wearing those shoes when we discovered her. I even found a witness who saw the delivery man drive off – they work at the Italian restaurant nearby – and they also saw Simone outside her studio, straight after the delivery guy left, walking back and forth for a minute, before going back inside."

"Maybe she was testing out her new shoes," Lauren mused.

"The delivery man's next customer was waiting to receive their new phone, and confirmed the guy delivered it on schedule. So I don't see how the delivery guy could have doubled back to kill Simone when I can't find any connection between them."

"What about Kayla's partner Troy?" Zoe suggested. "There's something about him I just don't like."

"I know what you mean." Lauren nodded.

"And they're top of my interview list," Mitch assured them.

The conversation turned to more pleasant topics, like the wedding.

Lauren told them about the cupcakes she was baking and decorating for the tower.

"It's not going to be too much work for you?" Mitch looked at her in concern.

"I'm sure I can manage," she replied with a smile.

"I've offered to help." Zoe turned to her cousin. "Just let me know."

"I will."

"Brrt!"

"I wish you *could* help, Annie," Lauren said. "But you're not allowed in the café kitchen, and that's where the big mixer is that I need – plus all the counter space."

"We'll have to practice walking down the aisle again next week," Zoe told her. "That will keep us busy."

"Brrt!"

After a satisfying dinner of steak and green salad, followed by carrot cupcakes Lauren had saved from the café that morning, they were ready to waltz.

Annie hopped onto the pink sofa, watching their antics with a curious gaze.

Zoe pressed a button on her phone, and strains of *The Blue Danube* filled the room.

Lauren looked up at Mitch and smiled. He held her hand in his, and placed his arm around her.

"Ready?" he whispered

"Yes."

They swept around the living room. Lauren wished it was bigger, but she let all her worries fall away and just enjoyed her time in Mitch's arms. She and Zoe passed each other, and she could tell Zoe was enjoying herself as well.

"Brrt," Annie called out in an encouraging manner as she passed by her.

"Phew!" Zoe grinned when the music faded.

"We should try *The Skaters' Waltz* now," Lauren suggested.

Zoe nodded, and hit a button on her phone.

The two couples waltzed around the room again – and again.

"I think we're pretty good," Chris observed after the music finished.

"That's what I thought." Zoe smiled at him.

"Maybe Simone was better at teaching the waltz than the paso doble," Mitch said thoughtfully.

"You could be right." Chris nodded.

After a little more practice, they decided to call it a night.

"Are you coming to church tomorrow?" she asked Mitch.

"Yes. I'll pick you up."

"I can make it, too," Chris said.

"Awesome!" Zoe grinned. "And after, Lauren and I are going to check on Mrs. Finch."

"Are you free for lunch?" Lauren asked Mitch.

"Definitely. Where would you like to go?"

"How about Gary's Burger Diner?" she suggested. Choices were limited in the small town.

"And *we* can go to the winery," Zoe told Chris.

"That sounds good." He smiled at her.

"Brrp?" Annie asked.

"I'll bring you back a plain patty from Gary's," Lauren promised.

"Brrt!" *Thank you.*

Lauren walked Mitch out. He held her in his arms and tenderly kissed her good night. Her spine tingled.

"I can't wait until we're man and wife." His voice was husky.

"Neither can I."

Against the backdrop of the dark night sky, with only the golden glow of the porchlight for illumination, he gave her a last, lingering kiss, then strode to his car.

Sighing softly, Lauren headed back into the house.

"I'll meet you here after we get back from Mrs. Finch's," Zoe was telling Chris.

"No problem."

Lauren thought that Chris's laid back, easy-going nature was the perfect foil for Zoe's impulsivity.

She entered the kitchen, wanting to give the two of them some privacy. Maybe Annie had the same thought, because she ambled in, joining her at the large pine table.

"Brrt?"

She jumped into Lauren's lap.

"Mitch is working hard at finding out who killed Simone," Lauren told her, "so we can all enjoy next Saturday – when I marry him."

Her fur baby snuggled into her lap.
"Brrp," she said sleepily.

CHAPTER 15

After church the next morning, Lauren and Zoe walked to Mrs. Finch's house, which was only a few blocks away.

Their elderly friend greeted them with a smile and assured them she was all right.

After a brief visit, they returned to Lauren's cottage.

"I'm going to get changed." Lauren exchanged her teal wrap dress for a more casual beige slacks and peach top ensemble. Her stomach grumbled – her breakfast had been brief as she'd been running a little late.

"I'm going to keep mine on." Zoe gestured to her black slacks and lavender top. "I think it looks good."

"It does." Lauren admired the outfit.

"Brrt?" Annie reminded her.

"Yes, I'll bring your lunch back." Lauren kissed the top of her furry head.

Mitch arrived, and Lauren hurried to greet him. He still wore his church attire of charcoal slacks and matching jacket.

"You look good." He surveyed her. "I like that peach color."

"Thanks. I thought my wrap dress might be a bit too formal for Gary's but since you're still wearing—"

"I didn't have time to change. Chris and I started talking to Father Mike and helped him tidy up the church after the congregation left – a little kid knocked a stack of bibles over when he hurried out." He chuckled.

She had a lovely time with Mitch at the burger place. A few customers said hello to them and chatted about the upcoming wedding.

After she enjoyed a smoky barbecue special, including a few fries and half a chocolate thick shake, she felt totally satisfied – not just with the food, but also with the company – her soon-to-be husband.

"What are you doing later today?" He captured her hand.

She told him about taking inventory for the wedding cupcakes.

"I can help you," he offered.

"Really?"

"I know we haven't spent much time together lately," he apologized. "I definitely want that to change."

"Me too," she replied softly.

"Then let's check out the ingredients at the café."

After giving Annie her plain burger patty, Lauren led him down the private hallway to the café.

"We need to check on flour, sugar, vanilla, eggs," she began. "And fondant for the decorations, but I think I ordered enough."

Mitch helped her tick off each item on her list.

"I'll ask Zoe to buy more supplies while we're on our honeymoon, so we'll be fully stocked when we re-open."

"I can't wait to walk along the beach with you." Mitch wrapped his arms around her and pulled her close.

"Me either." Her heart fluttered.

"We'll visit Annie every day with a video call."

"Thank you." She traced a finger down his cheek. How had she been so lucky to have met him?

"I know Zoe will take good care of her while we're gone."

"I know."

Lauren felt so happy, she didn't want to leave the cafe kitchen. But eventually, after tender, lingering kisses, Mitch said he still had a few boxes to pack.

"I can start bringing my stuff over tomorrow evening," he told her. "If that's a good time?"

"It is."

She floated back to the cottage, only to be brought up short by Zoe pacing and running a hand through her pixie cut, making the brunette strands spike up.

"What's wrong?" She stared at her cousin.

"I forgot about the place cards for the bistro!"

***

Zoe sank onto the sofa. "I've checked and rechecked my to-do list and thought I had everything under control, but just now, Annie tapped the screen with her paw to scroll down, and I noticed that I hadn't ticked off the place cards for the reception!"

Lauren sat down next to her.

"Brrt!" Annie hopped up between them, looking first at Lauren, then at Zoe.

"You're such a clever girl." Zoe stroked the feline's shoulder. "How could I have missed that?"

"You had a lot on your to-do list," Lauren pointed out. "Have I told you and Annie that you're the best co-maids of honor ever?"

"You haven't been married before." But Zoe looked a little cheerier.

"I know I'm lucky to have my two best friends walking down the aisle with me."

"Brrt!" Annie bunted her arm, asking for a pat. Lauren obliged.

"So where do we pick up these place cards?" Lauren asked, when

Zoe remained uncharacteristically silent.

"In Sacramento. Your mom wanted some fancy ones and we looked at the designs and agreed on—"

"That's right." With everything else that had been going on, she'd totally forgotten they'd worked out a seating plan a couple of weeks ago and ordered the cards.

"Let's pick them up tomorrow – the café will be closed, so we'll have plenty of time."

"I checked our online order and they're ready." Zoe gave her a little smile. "Thank you for not being upset."

They hung out at the cottage that evening. Annie wanted to watch the sequel to the princess movie again, and they obliged. Zoe microwaved a big bowl of popcorn, and they happily munched while they watched, Annie sitting on Lauren's lap, her gaze glued to the television screen.

***

"Let's go!" Zoe shifted from foot to foot by the back door the next morning.

"I'm coming." Lauren said goodbye to Annie and joined her cousin. "We'll be home later today."

"Brrt!" Annie ambled toward the living room.

They got into the car.

"So, we'll pick up these place cards, then what?" Zoe buckled her seatbelt as Lauren switched on the ignition.

"When does the bistro need them?"

"I was thinking we could give them to the manager when we have the rehearsal dinner Friday night."

"After we practice with Father Mike in the church."

"That's right. Annie and I need to try walking step-in-step again this week." Zoe giggled, then sobered. "I can't believe you're getting married."

"Sometimes I can't believe it either." Lauren swiftly glanced at her in reply, before focusing on the highway again.

They arrived in Sacramento, and Zoe directed her to the little print shop. There were other storefronts nearby, including a boutique.

"Look!" Zoe pointed through the windshield. "Isn't that where Kayla works?"

"Mitch did say the store she worked at was on this street." Lauren's eyes widened as she stared at the boutique boasting a mannequin wearing jeans and a posh diamond-checked sweater.

"After we pick up the cards, we can go in and grill her!" Zoe's brown eyes were alight with enthusiasm.

"If she's there, I'll call Mitch and let him know."

"That too." Zoe nodded.

They entered the print shop and picked up the place cards.

"They're beautiful." Lauren traced over the embossed gold lettering on the ivory cardstock.

She paid, tucking the receipt carefully into her wallet to give to her mother.

"They *are* gorgeous." Zoe sighed. "They even look better in real life than on the website, and they looked pretty good on there."

"I know." Lauren smiled at her bestie.

"Come on." Zoe touched her arm. "Let's check if Kayla is working today."

Lauren followed her into the small boutique, noticing there were a couple of pretty sweaters she wouldn't mind trying on. But Zoe zipped to the counter.

"Oh, hi, Kayla." Zoe sounded surprised and Lauren admired her cousin's acting skills.

"Do I know you?" The blonde girl wrinkled her brow for a second. "Oh, ballroom dancing lessons."

"That's right. We've had a lesson with Carol, and she's great, isn't she?"

"The best." Kayla nodded. "I really like her – so does my partner Troy. He says with her experience, there'll be no stopping us!"

"When we bumped into you coming out of Carol's studio, you were talking about how you heard she was hopeless. We wondered where you heard that? Because we didn't. Our friend in Gold Leaf Valley recommended Carol to us and said how good she was."

"Yeah, I've been trying to think who told me that." Kayla drummed her glittery purple fingertips on the counter. "I think it was our friend who was taking lessons with Simone. She said she heard that Carol was hopeless, because I asked her who we should go with – Simone or Carol. Since they're both in Zeke's Ridge, it didn't matter to me who taught me and Troy, as long as they were good and didn't cost too much – getting into ballroom can be expensive with the outfits and the lessons, but Troy says one day it will pay off when we're big-time champions."

"When did Simone tell you she could guarantee you could win or place in your first competition?" Lauren asked.

"At our first lesson with her." Kayla narrowed her eyes. "We'd taken some lessons here in the city, but it was getting too expensive, which was why we were looking around for another instructor, even if it meant we had to travel a bit."

"Where were you when Simone was killed?" Zoe asked casually, picking up a pair of blue earrings that dangled from a little rack on the counter.

"When was that?" Kayla asked.

"Last Tuesday, just before seven p.m."

"Oh, Troy and I were hanging out at his place."

"Where's that?" Lauren asked curiously.

"Here. In Sacramento."

"It's a bit of a drive from here to Zeke's Ridge for lessons," Zoe said.

"I know." Kayla nodded vigorously. "It takes up time we could spend either practicing more or just hanging out with friends, but ..." she hesitated, then leaned over the counter toward them. "Troy has a theory that as well as saving money on lessons, the instructors in smaller places like Zeke's Ridge will be grateful to have us as students, and might give us more time in our lesson – for free. So instead of one hour, we get an extra ten or fifteen minutes most of the time, because the instructor doesn't have students straight after us."

"Has that worked so far?" Lauren asked.

"No." Kayla made a face. "Troy even asked Simone for extra free time just before our competition, but she laughed it off and said we were totally ready and didn't need it." She scowled. "She was wrong."

"Yeah." Zoe took a step back when Kayla's expression darkened more.

"We shouldn't take up any more of your time," Lauren said.

"Do you want those earrings?" Kayla pointed to the baubles in Zoe's hand.

"Oops. Sorry." Zoe placed them back on the jewelry rack. "I was tempted, but I don't think they're really me."

When they were near the entrance, Zoe whispered to her, "Let's skedaddle. I think she's still scowling at me because I didn't buy anything."

Lauren let out a deep breath when they reached the sidewalk.

"Phew!" Zoe shook her head. "I thought Kayla's partner was a little scary but …"

"I know," Lauren agreed. But what had Kayla done, really? She'd answered their questions and asked a reasonable one in return when Zoe had continued to clutch the earrings.

"I need to call Mitch." She pulled her phone out of her purse and quickly told him where they were and that they'd just spoken to Kayla.

"Thanks. I'll call the store right now and ask her to stay until I can get over there." After promising he'd see her that evening, he said goodbye.

"Well?" Zoe asked impatiently.

Lauren gave her the gist of the conversation.

Zoe sighed. "What are we going to do now?"

"Go home? Is there anything else on your to-do list?"

Zoe dug her purse out of her jeans' pocket and checked her phone, making a show of scrolling down, a rueful smile on her face.

"Nope. Oh – yeah."

"What is it?"

"Visit our favorite ice cream place before we go home." She winked.

CHAPTER 16

After a fortifying maple-rhubarb ice cream for Lauren, and green tea and fig for Zoe, they headed home.

"I don't think much of Kayla's alibi." Zoe wrinkled her nose. "Anyone can say they were hanging out at their dance partner's house. I wonder if they're romantically involved?"

"I wasn't sure about that, either," Lauren replied. "They could be."

"Yeah." Zoe nodded. "Otherwise, why are they spending so much time with each other when they're not dancing?"

"Because they like each other?" Lauren suggested.

"I wonder if they're magic on the dance floor like Carol and her partner were," Zoe mused. "Maybe not, because they didn't win a prize in their competition."

"Because Simone taught them the wrong moves," Lauren pointed out.

"True. So they really do have a motive for killing Simone. They're mad because they paid her for lessons, she taught them incorrectly *and* made them lose at the competition."

"I'm sure Mitch will find out if they were together that night," Lauren said. "Maybe a neighbor saw them going inside or they ordered pizza or something."

"Good point." Zoe glanced at her, a big smile on her face. "We make a great team."

"We do."

***

On the way home, they stopped at Mrs. Finch's house to show her the place cards. After she enthused over them, they made her a latte using her capsule machine, before heading to the cottage.

"Brrt!" Annie ran to greet them.

"Look." Lauren fished out one of the cards and showed it to her. "They have everyone's names on them, so they know where to sit at the reception."

"Brrt?" Annie gently patted the gold embossing.

"Yes, we have one for you." Lauren rifled through the cards before finding one with her fur baby's name on it.

"It says Annie," Zoe said helpfully. "See?"

"You'll be at our table." Lauren held it in front of the feline.

"Brrp." *Thank you.*

Annie was attending the first part of the reception, and then she and Mitch planned to take her home. The bistro was on the outskirts of Gold Leaf Valley, so it wouldn't take long to bring her fur baby back to the cottage and then return to the guests.

"Mitch is coming over tonight," Lauren reminded her cousin. "He's bringing some of his stuff over."

"Oops." A guilty look crossed Zoe's face. "I haven't done anything about packing up my things to move into his apartment."

"There's plenty of time." Lauren touched her arm. "If you change your mind and want to keep living here, you know that's okay."

"Thanks." Zoe smiled at her. "But I don't want to cramp your style."

"You'll have plenty of time to pack while we're in Hawaii."

"True." Zoe nodded. "And Chris said he would help."

"Good."

Lauren made some room in her closet for Mitch's clothes, wondering if there would be enough space. She eyed the dresser – should they buy another one? She'd made one drawer available for him, but would he need more than that? It would be something they'd have to discuss.

When Mitch came over that evening, he carried a few boxes into her bedroom.

"What's in them?" she asked.

"Stuff," he replied easily. "And some clothes. I thought I'd bring the rest of it over in a few days' time – and I've already packed my suitcase for our honeymoon."

"Did you speak to Kayla?"

"Yeah." His mouth firmed. "So far I haven't been able to find any proof that she and her partner were together that evening – just their word."

"No delivery driver bringing takeout?"

"No. They said they were watching a ballroom dancing movie and practicing some of the moves. I'll track down her partner tomorrow and ask him some questions." There was a determined look on his face.

They enjoyed an easy dinner of leftovers, Zoe joining them. Then Mitch made his apologies and left, saying he had an early start in the morning.

"I'm going to be at the warehouse where Kayla's partner Troy works as soon as it opens," he vowed.

After Mitch left, Zoe let out a sigh.

"I guess that means we don't get to grill Troy ourselves tomorrow."

"Not during our opening hours," Lauren replied.

"How's it going with the fondant flowers and cupcake tower?" Zoe's eyes widened, as if she'd just remembered those to-do items.

"I'll be busy this week with them," Lauren reminded her.

"Hmm. Maybe this time Mitch will be the one to catch the killer – instead of us."

"He *is* good at his job," Lauren reminded her.

"I know." Zoe sighed. "But you know I love sleuthing and finding out who the bad guy is."

"I do." Lauren nodded.

"Brrt!"

***

The next day, Mitch strode into the café just before the lunch rush.

"I spoke to Kayla's partner Troy," he told her.

She held up a cardboard cup, and he nodded.

"And?" Zoe was also behind the counter.

When Annie had spied him entering, she'd trotted up to greet him. Now, with her ears pricked, she appeared to listen as well.

"His alibi matches Kayla's. He got the name of the movie right and said they stayed in all evening. And they didn't order any food."

"Pooh." Zoe frowned.

"Yeah." Mitch looked like he was suppressing a chuckle. "That just about sums it up. I canvassed the neighbors in the street, but none of them saw either Kayla or Troy leaving the house." He furrowed his brow. "Not that anyone saw them arrive there."

"So they could have killed Simone just before seven p.m. and driven back to Sacramento, which would take about eighty minutes," Zoe commented, "and then gone to Troy's house, and watched that ballroom dancing movie."

"Pretty much." Mitch nodded. "I'm going to Zeke's Ridge next, to canvass again – maybe someone saw Troy's car parked near Simone's studio – it's distinctive with its beat-up appearance and yellow sticker. Although they both told me they didn't have a lesson with Simone the day she died."

"What about Detective Castern?" Lauren asked. "Can't he go to Zeke's Ridge?"

"I don't trust him to be competent. Especially in this case." He shook his head. "He'd probably be delighted if my vacation time was postponed because the killer was still at large."

She studied the slight shadows under her fiancé's eyes. "You're not working too hard, are you?"

"Yeah," he admitted with a wry smile. "I want to get this case solved so we can enjoy our wedding – and honeymoon." The intimate light in his eyes made her blush.

"So what can we do to help?" Zoe asked.

"Brrt?"

"Keep going with the wedding preparations. You've got your bachelorette party on Thursday, right?"

"And you've got your bachelor party," Lauren reminded him.

"It will be more like a quiet get together with my friends," he assured her.

"Same here," she replied.

"Are you sure about that, Lauren?" Zoe winked at her.

"I hope you don't have something outrageous in mind," Lauren warned her.

"Brrt!"

"Don't worry. I was only teasing." Zoe giggled. "We've got the rehearsal dinner on Friday with Aunt Celia and your folks." She glanced at Mitch. "Lauren will be perfectly presentable."

"Good." He smiled tenderly at Lauren. "My parents are arriving on Thursday and staying at my place, so I'll be at Chris's from then until Saturday."

They exchanged a loving glance, then Lauren handed him his latte.

"Thanks. I'd better get going. I'll call you later."

Lauren watched him stride out of the café. She hoped the killer was behind bars by Friday night.

CHAPTER 17

That afternoon, Mitch called, frustration in his tone.

"No one noticed Troy's beat-up black car in the vicinity when Simone was killed. It looks like it's back to the drawing board."

"I'm sorry," Lauren commiserated.

They spoke for a few more minutes about the case.

"I'll try to bring some more boxes over tonight," he said, before ending the call.

"Well?" Zoe's eyebrows rose. "What did he say?"

Lauren repeated the conversation.

"Who could be the killer?" Zoe tapped her cheek. "Carol, Kayla, or her partner Troy?"

"Or someone we don't know about." Lauren crinkled her brow. "Surely Simone had more students than just us and Kayla and her partner."

"You'd think so," Zoe agreed. "Didn't Celeste at the bridal shop say she had brides complaining about taking lessons from Simone?"

"Unless word of mouth got around that if they didn't want to be let down on the dance floor, then they shouldn't take lessons from Simone," Lauren slowly suggested.

"Or if they didn't want Simone stealing their bridegrooms," Zoe added.

"Brrt!"

***

They were just about to close up that afternoon, when Carol entered. Luckily, Lauren hadn't turned off the espresso machine.

"Did I make it in time?" Carol asked hopefully.

"Just!" Zoe's voice was dramatic.

"I was driving home from Sacramento and thought I'd stop for a large latte hit." Carol yawned, hiding her mouth with the palm of her hand. "It's been a busy day."

"Oh?" Lauren asked, the machine grinding the beans with a growling noise.

"Celeste from the bridal shop called, asking if I had any business cards to give her. Now that Simone's – dead – she has panicked brides calling and asking her for last minute dance teacher suggestions. I think I have you two to thank for that. She said you'd recommended me to her."

"You're welcome." Zoe grinned. "We really enjoyed our lesson with you."

"Except we haven't done any practicing this week yet," Lauren said guiltily.

"I'm sure you'll squeeze in a little time before the big day. It's Saturday, isn't it?"

"Yes," Lauren replied.

"I can't believe we got taken in by Simone." Zoe shook her head. "Maybe she just wasn't as good as she thought she was."

"I'm surprised she taught Kayla and her partner Troy the wrong moves in the paso doble." Carol tsked. "But that's what happens when you don't really know what you're doing. You make things up." She leaned across the counter as Lauren steamed the milk. "It makes me wonder if she was even properly trained."

Lauren created a peacock on the surface of the micro foam while she listened.

"It seems a shame to cover that gorgeous design with a lid," Carol remarked.

"Can we get you a cupcake to go?" Zoe asked. "We have one lavender or a triple chocolate ganache left."

"Why don't I buy both of them?" There was a twinkle in Carol's eye. "Treat myself."

"Good idea." Zoe used the tongs and carefully placed the goodies into a brown paper bag.

"Brrt?" Annie joined them from her cat basket, where she'd been snoozing. Her eyes were alert as she studied Carol.

"I'm just about to go home," Carol told the feline. "I've had a long day." She stifled a yawn. "I'm sure your latte will help, Lauren." She picked up the cup and the cupcake bag. "Oh, did you find out who owned that blue ribbon I found outside the other day? I thought later on maybe it belonged to a little girl who lost it."

"It did," Lauren replied. "She was thrilled when we gave it to her." She thought back, remembering when Carol found the hair decoration that she'd called it blue then too, when it had looked like purple to Lauren, and Claire had called it purple as well.

"That color might be cute for a child, but I didn't think much of it on Simone's shoes – blue swirls! Really, she should have shown more decorum in her outfits."

Lauren froze. She felt Zoe stand stock-still behind her. They risked a glance at each other.

"Her shoes?" Zoe asked after a moment. "What about her shoes?"

"Those ugly swirls of color she had on them. Really, what sort of professional would wear ballroom dancing shoes with blue swirls?"

"But they were purple swirls," Lauren said slowly.

"Brrt?" Annie's fur started to rise.

"How would you know that Simone was wearing her new shoes that day – the day she was killed?" Zoe tensed.

"She told us they were coming," Lauren remembered. "She was very specific."

"Yeah." Zoe nodded. "She said they were arriving by special delivery at six p.m. and she described them to us, including the purple swirls on them."

"But that color looked like blue to you, didn't it?" Lauren asked Carol. "Just like you called Molly's ribbon blue, when in fact it's purple."

"So I got the colors mixed up." Carol shrugged, and turned for the door. "I'm getting older; it happens."

"You're color blind," Zoe stated.

"So?" Carol walked toward the door.

"How did you know Simone's shoes arrived that day?" Lauren started to come around the counter, her heart hammering. But how could she let Carol escape?

Carol paused, then turned around. She sighed. "If you must know, I went over to her studio because I had another student cancelling on me. I figured she had something to do with it."

"And when you saw her there, wearing her new shoes, maybe boasting about them? Did you tell Mitch you were over there just before she was killed?" Lauren pressed.

Carol dropped her pleasant expression, her eyes becoming cold.

"Mitch told us the time of Simone's death was just before seven p.m. because we found her when we arrived at our lesson at seven. And the delivery driver was due to arrive at six. In fact, Mitch tracked down the delivery driver, and verified that he'd delivered those shoes right on time, and got to his next destination on schedule." Zoe's gaze zeroed in on Carol. "And there was a witness who saw him leave Simone's studio, and then saw Simone alive and well."

"Simone had time to try on the shoes before *you* got there," Lauren added. "In fact, maybe she was testing them when she was spotted outside her studio."

"Brrt!" Annie stared intently at Carol.

"You think you're all so clever," Carol replied. "Why couldn't you have left this alone? We could have been friends. You said you loved my waltzing lesson."

"We did," Lauren admitted.

"Yeah. But I don't think I can be friends with a killer." Zoe's tone softened a little. "I'm sorry. I thought you were great."

"So did I," Lauren confessed.

"You have no proof I killed Simone," Carol said.

"Other than being there right before she was murdered," Lauren stated. "And lying about your alibi."

Carol flushed a bright red. Her fingers clenched on the cupcake bag and the cardboard coffee cup.

"I'm going to call Mitch." Lauren put her hand in her capris' pocket to pull out her phone.

"Don't!" Carol held out the hand containing the cupcakes. "You don't understand. I *had* to kill her. She was destroying me."

"How?" Zoe asked.

Lauren's hand froze in her pocket.

"When Simone set up her studio in Zeke's Ridge, she wasn't getting many students. So she started badmouthing me, telling anyone who would listen that I was a terrible teacher, and a fraud! She even said that my trophies were forgeries!" Carol heaved a breath.

"And they're not?" Lauren guessed.

"No." Carol shook her head. "They're the real deal – *I'm* the real deal. Simone was the fraud. Her trophies were fake. Did you ever take a good look at them?"

"Not really," Zoe admitted.

"For instance, her trophy that said Best Dance Teacher California 2019 – did you notice that it just said California and not a specific town or dance studio? I did a little digging and realized I was dealing with someone who was ruthless, moved around a lot – and not a great teacher. There was no record she won any of those trophies, even the ballroom dancing ones. She was okay with the basics, but you saw what she did to Kayla and her partner Troy. She taught them the wrong moves, and got them in trouble with the judges when she guaranteed them they'd at least place. No teacher can guarantee that, unless she has an "in" with the judges."

"You believed Kayla and Troy when they said she promised them they'd do well at the competition?" Lauren asked.

"Yes." Carol nodded. "Why would they lie? I've set them straight about that, so even if they decide not to continue with me, they have more of an idea of what to look out for in a *real* dance instructor.

"But why did you kill her?" Zoe pressed.

"Because she started taunting me – again. I'd marched over there and told her this time I meant it: she had to stop telling lies about me. I was *just* making a living with my teaching – I don't like charging too much, because I'm worried people can't afford it, but when she muscled in on my business, my finances started going downhill. Luckily, I own my little studio – I bought it years ago and eventually paid it off – but the rent has gone up on my house and at the rate I'm going, I'll have to break the lease and move into the studio.

"Simone laughed. She said she could do whatever she wanted, and what was I going to do to stop her? She suggested I retire, so she could have my few remaining students. And she said to make it snappy, before she started another rumor about me, this time even worse." Carol sniffed. "I don't know what could be worse than saying I was a bad teacher, when I've always prided myself on being the best instructor possible."

"Then what?" Zoe asked, her eyes wide.

"Brrt?" Annie added.

"I picked up one of her *fake* trophies, ready to hit her on the head, and she turned pale. Suddenly, she seemed to shrink in on herself and she admitted those trophies were phony. Ha! I knew it! But it was too late. I just thought of what she'd just threatened me with, and what she'd already done to me, and BAM!"

Zoe paled.

"And then you went back to your studio and watched TV," Lauren guessed.

"Exactly. It was a re-run, so I remembered some of the plot, and watched the rest of it, although I found it hard to focus on it. I was shaking."

"Did you wait for the delivery driver to leave before you went over there?" Lauren asked.

"No – I had no idea she was getting those stupid shoes. Trust Simone to trip me up somehow." Carol frowned. "The street was quiet at that time –

maybe that's why nobody saw me." She shook her head. "But now you know why I did what I did, surely you can understand?" She lifted her shoulders in a plea. "I'm not a bad person. This is the first time I've ever done something that wasn't good."

"I'm sorry," Lauren said as gently as she could. "I need to call Mitch."

"Maybe he can get you a special deal," Zoe suggested.

"I know he'll listen to you," Lauren offered.

"No!" Carol turned for the door. "I won't be arrested!"

"Brrt!" Annie leaped in the air, and knocked the cupcake bag out of her hand.

"Ahhh!" Carol stumbled, her hand holding the coffee cup hitting the counter. The lid came off, hot liquid gushing over her hand.

"Oww! It's burning!" Carol jiggled from one foot to the other, waving her fingers in the air. "Arghhh!"

"Here!" Zoe threw a mug of cold water over Carol's hand, but some of it splashed onto her face.

Lauren speed-dialed Mitch while Zoe kept throwing more cold water on Carol, until she was eventually soaked.

"Brrt!" Annie approved, jumping onto a table to keep a better eye on the dance instructor – and killer.

When Mitch arrived, he handcuffed a defeated Carol, who'd started to cry. But it was hard to tell, with water dripping all over her and onto the floor.

CHAPTER 18

The next evening, the five of them had dinner at the cottage. Lauren had saved some pides from the café, and they enjoyed those while Mitch updated them.

Annie had already eaten her meal of beef in gravy, and now sat next to Lauren at the kitchen table, while Mitch sat on Lauren's other side.

"Carol confessed to everything at the station," Mitch informed them.

"What will happen to her?" Chris asked.

"She'll be going away, but she might be able to get a deal if she retains a good lawyer. She said she feels terrible about what she did, but at that moment, she didn't see any other option."

They were silent for a moment.

"Brrt?" Annie bunted Lauren's hand.

"Thank you for helping us with Carol," she told her fur baby.

"Yeah, if you hadn't knocked her off balance with the cupcake bag, making her spill her latte, I mightn't have thought of dousing her with water," Zoe praised the feline.

"Brrt!" *Thank you!*

"Now Simone's death has been resolved, we can focus on the wedding." Mitch looked tenderly at Lauren. "My folks are arriving tomorrow and I'll be moving in with Chris until the wedding."

"And the bachelorette party is tomorrow night," Zoe added. "I hope we don't get too wild and crazy at Mrs. Finch's." She looked teasingly at Chris.

"Our evening is going to be low key," Chris told Mitch. "Ed, Father Mike, and a couple of your old buddies."

"Good." Mitch nodded. "We've got the rehearsal dinner on Friday, then the ceremony on Saturday. I want to be in good shape for both." He pressed a kiss on Lauren's hair. "Saturday is going to be the most important day of my life."

"Ohh." Lauren blinked back tears. "Mine too." She smiled at him.

"How are the cupcakes coming along?" Zoe asked. "For the tower?"

"I'll be baking nonstop on Friday," Lauren replied. "And tomorrow I'll work on the fondant flowers."

"Let me know if I can help," Zoe offered.

"What about your pottery mugs?" Chris asked.

"All ready to take to the bistro." Zoe beamed. "And the café mugs are ready as well. Now all I have to do is practice walking down the aisle again with Annie."

"What about a quick waltz practice tonight?" Lauren glanced at everyone.

"Good idea." Zoe's eyes sparkled.

The guys nodded in approval.

"Brrt!" *Yes!*

***

The next day, Zoe was kept busy with customers as Lauren stole every spare moment she could to make the decorations for the cupcake tower. She'd started one hour earlier than usual, baked the usual amount of treats for the café, but realized at lunchtime she'd have to spend more time that evening making the fondant flowers. She hoped she wasn't going to be late for her own bachelorette party!

But it would all be worth it, she assured herself, smiling at Ed as he rolled out pastry for his light, flaky Danishes.

"Let me know if you need any help with your doodads," he said gruffly, nodding to the array of pink flowers on her work surface.

"Thanks. But I think I can do it. I'll be in here early tomorrow to make the cakes for the tower."

"Why not take a break from making your usual supply for the café tomorrow? I can make more pastries instead."

"That would be great." Lauren smiled at him. Mitch, Zoe, and Chris had expressed concern last night that she was trying to do too much with all the baking for the wedding, and just now, she realized they were right. Zoe might kill her – although that was a bad choice of words – if she was late to her own bachelorette party. And she didn't want to be too tired to enjoy it.

She also wanted to say hello to Mitch's parents when they arrived today.

Knowing Ed would take care of the café baking tomorrow spurred her on, and by the time five o'clock arrived, she was almost finished making the decorations.

"They look amazing!" Zoe came through the swinging kitchen doors and gazed at the fondant flowers arrayed on the work surface. Ed had gone home, although he'd stayed later than usual to help with the dishes, so it was just the two of them.

Annie was in the café space, as cats weren't allowed in the commercial kitchen – even Annie.

"Thanks." Lauren gave her a relieved smile.

"Mitch called when you didn't answer your phone."

"I turned it off a few hours ago so I wouldn't be distracted," Lauren replied, suddenly feeling guilty she'd done so.

"He said his parents can't wait to see you." Zoe grinned "They know we're having the bachelorette party tonight, so they just wanted to say a quick hello to you."

"How do I look?" Lauren took off her apron.

"Awesome! Well, like a bride-to-be who's been working all day."

"Better?" She patted her hair into place.

"A bit," Zoe admitted. "Come on, we've got the bachelorette party as well."

"What about Annie?"

"She's waiting in the café for you." Zoe grinned, then her face fell. "With everything that's happened this week, we haven't practiced walking down the aisle again. Maybe we should do it at breakfast tomorrow."

"Good idea. Because we've got the rehearsal tomorrow afternoon."

"And we're even closing the café two hours early." Zoe giggled. "I know you don't like doing that."

"But it's for the best reason in the world." Lauren smiled softly. "Getting ready to marry Mitch."

***

Lauren enjoyed meeting Mitch's parents once more, then made her apologies as Zoe dragged her off to get ready for her bachelorette party.

Mitch's folks said they'd try Gary's Burger Diner for dinner, as they'd heard good things about it from Mitch and Chris.

Lauren wore her teal wrap dress, while Zoe donned a black and white pantsuit with zigzags down the sides. The trio drove to Mrs. Finch's house.

"Brooke is going to be there, and Claire, as well as Martha, and Ms. Tobin," Lauren told her fur baby, parking in front of their friend's

Victorian cottage. A few other cars were parked nearby.

"Brooke's here already!" Zoe pointed to their friend's vehicle.

"We're not late, are we?" Lauren cast her cousin a worried glance.

"Right on time."

"Brrt!" *Good!*

The party went off without a hitch. As well as their local friends, Zoe had secretly organized the arrival of two of Lauren's old friends from Sacramento who she'd lost touch with. When Lauren saw them, tears came to her eyes and she hugged Zoe.

"Thank you," she whispered.

"That's what co-maids of honor are for." Zoe winked. "Isn't that right, Annie?"

"Brrt!"

Everyone made a fuss of Annie, as well as Mrs. Finch, and Martha. Lauren kept an eye on her elderly friends, making sure they had everything they needed.

As another surprise, Zoe had ordered pizza for the party, including

Lauren, and Zoe specials. That typical Zoe touch made Lauren laugh, but she had to admit it was practical.

"Don't worry about fitting into your gown on Saturday," Zoe murmured to her. "A little pizza won't hurt at all."

"I think you're right," Lauren agreed, enjoying her first mouthful. She'd practically skipped lunch that day because she'd been so busy making the fondant flowers.

After a wonderful night, they eventually went home, Mrs. Finch assuring them she'd be there at the wedding – the senior center was doing a special pick up of the guests, initiated by Martha. Lauren made a mental note to thank her at the wedding.

***

The next morning, Zoe hummed the *Wedding March* while holding a piece of whole-wheat toast in one hand and Annie's lead in the other. She and Annie practiced walking down the aisle – or in this case, walking down the hallway.

"Now you come after us, Lauren," Zoe instructed.

Lauren obeyed, clutching her granola bowl. "You two are definitely in step together. Annie, you're amazing."

"Brrt!" *Thank you.* She turned around to give Lauren a happy look.

"What about me?" Zoe joked.

"You too." Lauren nodded.

"I wonder how the guys' night went?" Zoe pondered. Her phone buzzed and she pulled it out of her jeans' pocket. She giggled. "It's as if Chris has read my mind."

Lauren's phone suddenly vibrated and she stared at the screen.

"Did Chris send you a copy of this?" She showed Zoe the photo of Mitch and Chris taking a selfie in front of Chris's house.

"Yep." Zoe grinned. "It looks like they had a tame night as well. No shaved heads or anything."

"Mitch did say there wouldn't be anything untoward, and Father Mike was attending as well."

Zoe nodded.

"I have to go." Lauren checked her watch with a start. "I've got all those cupcakes to make!"

"We'll be right behind you," Zoe called after her.

"Brrt!"

CHAPTER 19

Lauren wondered a few times that day if her decision to make the cupcake tower herself was wise, but when all the cupcakes were baked, frosted, and decorated with the fondant flowers, she had to admit she was proud of her work.

"They look great," Ed said gruffly that afternoon. He'd finished cleaning the kitchen and was about to leave. "I guess I'll see you tomorrow at the church."

"Yes." Lauren smiled. "I hope you enjoy your time off next week." She was giving Zoe and Ed paid vacation time while she was on her honeymoon.

"I'll be helping out at the shelter a lot." His white teeth flashed briefly. "Rebecca will be there, too. I'll take AJ as well." His Maine Coon often accompanied him to the shelter and had made friends with some of the cats there.

"Does she want to come to the wedding tomorrow, since Annie will be there?" Lauren asked, realizing she hadn't thought of that before.

"Thanks, but I think she'd prefer to stay at home. But I thought I could record the ceremony with my phone, so she could watch it later, and see Annie being co-maid of honor."

"That would be great," Lauren replied. "My mother has hired a videographer but the video won't be ready until after we get back from our honeymoon. Mrs. Snuggle might be interested in watching your recording as well."

"I'll discuss it with Father Mike." Ed grinned briefly.

After he departed, Lauren sat down for a moment.

"Let's go." Zoe zoomed in through the swinging kitchen doors. "It's three o'clock, and I've locked up."

"We've got to clean up."

"I'd say you've already done that in here." Zoe glanced around the gleaming kitchen.

"It was mostly Ed."

"He's a good guy. Okay, let's quickly tidy up in the café and then we're off to the church to rehearse at four-thirty."

Annie was already sniffing in the corners, checking for anything left behind.

"Brrt!" She scampered over to Lauren.

She picked up the silver-gray tabby.

"I know," she whispered into her furry ear. "I can't believe I'm getting married tomorrow."

"Brrp," Annie whispered back in approval.

They quickly stacked the pine chairs onto the table, then Zoe got the vacuum out while Lauren tidied everything away behind the counter, and checked the money in the register, making a mental note to ask Zoe to bank it next week – something else she'd forgotten about in the build-up to the ceremony tomorrow.

When the café gleamed, she looked around with a smile. Her coffee shop – no, hers, Annie's, and

Zoe's – looked like it was already waiting for them to return and fill it with customers, cupcakes, and the enticing scent of coffee. And they would.

They trooped through the private hallway to the cottage, and changed quickly – Lauren in her plum wrap dress and Zoe in slacks and a lavender top. Annie stood patiently while she was buckled into her harness.

"Let's skedaddle." Zoe held out Lauren's car keys.

They zoomed off to the church. There were cars parked there already, including Mitch's.

"He's here," Lauren whispered.

"And so are his folks." Zoe nudged her.

They stood outside the white clapboard church, along with her own parents, and Father Mike.

"Ready for tomorrow?" Her mother looked at her fondly.

"We definitely are, Aunt Celia." Zoe answered for her.

"Hello, Annie," her mom greeted the feline.

"Brrt!"

Lauren nodded, and gave her mom and dad a warm smile. Then she greeted Mitch's parents – and Mitch.

"Where's Chris?" Zoe frowned, looking at her phone.

"I'm here," came his voice from behind her. "Sorry, I got held up."

Zoe smiled at him.

Father Mike cleared his throat. "If everyone's ready, we can begin the rehearsal."

Although it wasn't the actual ceremony, butterflies filled Lauren's stomach as she walked down the aisle on her father's arm behind Zoe and Annie. She felt overwhelmed for a minute, but was still able to notice her co-maids of honor were perfectly in step.

When she reached Mitch's side, she looked up at him, taken aback for a second by the love in his eyes.

Amazingly, Lauren didn't stumble when she said "I do," which she hoped was a good omen for the actual ceremony.

After the run through, they thanked Father Mike, and promised to see him that night at the rehearsal dinner.

"I wouldn't miss it." He smiled. "Thank you for inviting me."

The rehearsal dinner was successful. Fortunately, Lauren's mother approved of the food and atmosphere at the bistro, since the reception was going to be held there the next day.

Lauren brought Annie to spend a few minutes with everyone before taking her back home – a test run for tomorrow when she would be at the reception for a little while – unless so many guests were too overwhelming for her.

Mitch's parents also approved – Mitch and Lauren had organized the dinner, as his folks lived in San Diego.

"I just know tomorrow is going to be perfect, Lauren," her mother told her fondly.

"Definitely," Zoe chimed in.

The dinner ended early, Lauren's mother urging her to get a decent amount of sleep.

"You don't want to have shadows under your eyes on your big day," she told her daughter.

"I guess Brooke could cover them with makeup." Zoe winked.

***

"I feel sick." Lauren touched her stomach, the satin fabric of her gown smooth under her fingertips.

"Brrt?" Annie peered at her in concern, the flowered headband of pink gerberas, roses, and orchids, making her look like royalty.

"Do you want me to stop the car for a minute?" Her father patted her hand.

Her mother had gone ahead in the limousine first, before sending it back to the cottage for the four of them.

"Maybe we should," Zoe agreed. "You don't want to ruin your beautiful gown."

Lauren drew in a deep breath, the nerves easing for a second. "I think I'll be fine."

"That's the spirit," her dad said in relief.

"Yeah, marrying Mitch can't be nearly as scary as facing down a killer."

She started laughing. Zoe's comment put everything into perspective. "Thank you."

"You look beautiful," Zoe said after a moment.

"Brooke did a great job with the hair and makeup." Lauren nodded.

"No – it's something else – it's you," Zoe told her.

She blinked back unbidden tears. "And *you* look amazing," she told her cousin, admiring the champagne pantsuit and the subtle makeup Brooke had added to highlight Zoe's attractive features. She'd also fluffed up her pixie cut.

"Brrt?"

"Of course, you look gorgeous too, Annie. Just like a real princess." She stroked her fur baby's silver-gray coat. "And Dad, you look very smart in that suit."

"Thank you." He smiled.

The gleaming white limousine pulled up outside the church.

"Ready?" her father asked.

She took a deep breath. "Ready."

"I think Annie and I were born ready!" Zoe helped Annie out of the vehicle.

Zoe's phone buzzed and she fished it out of her tiny champagne purse. "Chris wants you to know that Mitch is here and he can't wait to see you walk down the aisle."

A feeling of serene contentment settled over her. The attack of nerves was forgotten.

"Let's go." She remembered Celeste from the bridal shop mentioning that some brides galloped down the aisle – she definitely didn't want to do that, but she did want to marry Mitch – the only man for her.

Zoe and Annie walked ahead of her, Annie turning around, as if to make sure that Lauren followed. She smiled at her fur baby, and took her father's arm.

The Victorian church looked like it belonged on a postcard with its steeple, and stained-glass windows sparkling in the late afternoon sun.

The strains of the *Wedding March* filled the church as she entered. All the guests oohed and ahhed when they spied Zoe and Annie walking perfectly in step, side by side.

Lauren saw her mom look approvingly at her co-maids of honor, then she saw Mitch standing next to Chris, with Father Mike looking solemn yet joyous.

Molly was there with her mom Claire, and her dad. The little girl wore a pink and white party dress and squirmed in her seat in order to get a better look at Zoe and Annie.

"Annie!" She waved at the feline.

"Brrt!" Annie replied, glancing at her happily, but not breaking her perfectly matching stride with Zoe's.

The congregation stood as Lauren glided down the aisle, her heart full of love for Mitch – and everyone in the church.

Martha and her friend Iris were in attendance, also Mrs. Finch. Zoe's, Mitch's, and Chris's parents were there, along with Ed, Hans, Ms. Tobin, Brooke and Jeff, and all their friends and family. Ed discreetly held his phone; Lauren guessed he was filming the ceremony for AJ and Mrs. Snuggle.

When she reached Mitch's side, he drew in a breath. "You look even more beautiful than usual," he whispered.

"So do you." She took in his classic gray morning suit with blue tie, and crisp white shirt. The devastating combination made him look even more handsome.

Chris stood next to him, looking attractive in his gray morning suit.

"I'm very proud to marry you two," Father Mike told them, beaming.

Lauren spoke her vows in a clear and confident voice – so did Mitch.

When he slid the gleaming gold ring on her finger, she smiled up at him. The love in his eyes filled her soul.

Father Mike declared them man and wife, and they kissed briefly – a tender, intimate kiss.

When she turned to smile at Zoe and Annie, who had stood so patiently throughout the ceremony, there was a look of wonder in Zoe's eyes.

"I have to ask Chris something." She walked over to him, took his hands in hers, and murmured to him.

Surprise and pleasure crossed his face, and he nodded enthusiastically.

Beaming, Zoe zipped over to Father Mike and whispered to him, then rushed over to Lauren and Mitch.

"Lauren, will you be mad if I marry Chris right now?"

"Brrp?" Annie looked up at her co-maid of honor with wide green eyes.

Lauren was tempted to repeat her fur baby's comment.

"Watching you and Mitch get married made me *really* realize that Chris is the guy for me. And this is the perfect moment. Everyone is here that I'd invite to my own wedding, and Annie and you – hopefully – could be my co-maids of honor – or is that matron and maid?" Zoe's brow furrowed for a second. "And the reception at the bistro is exactly what Chris and I would choose for ourselves if we got married in the future – so why not now?"

Lauren looked at Mitch, who looked like he was stifling a chuckle. He gave Chris a thumbs up. Chris returned the gesture with a grateful smile.

"And this outfit," Zoe rushed on, smoothing a hand over her sleek pants leg. "I just *love* it. I know I wouldn't be able to find anything I'd like better. And Father Mike is here, and I know I want him to marry us, and—"

"Yes. I mean no," she added hastily when she saw her cousin's look of confusion. "I won't be mad. It's such a Zoe thing to do – what could be more perfect at my – our –wedding?"

"I don't want you to think I'm high-jacking your day." But Zoe looked relieved.

"You're not," Lauren assured her. "You and Annie are my best friends – who better to share today with? And I'm so happy for you and Chris." She hugged her cousin. "I've always thought he was the one for you."

"Thanks." Zoe quickly blinked back tears, then turned to the priest. "We're ready, Father—"

"I want to be a pwincess!" Molly's voice sounded throughout the church. "Lauren, Zoe, and Annie are. Why can't I be, Mommy?"

Claire attempted to shush her, but Zoe's face lit up even more. "Can we include her?" she asked softly.

"Yes." Lauren nodded, tears now coming to *her* eyes.

Zoe zipped down the aisle, and spoke to Molly and Claire. Molly nodded vigorously and clambered over her mom to join Zoe.

"Thank you," Claire said in a heart-felt tone. "I don't think she'll ever forget this."

"We'll be princesses together," Zoe promised the little girl.

"Really?" Molly's face was one huge smile.

"Yes." Lauren had joined them, Annie by her side. "But we're all going to have to walk down the aisle again."

"Goody!" Molly clapped her hands in delight.

When the strains of the *Wedding March* sounded once more, Molly and Annie appeared first. Molly carefully held Annie's leash, and half walked, half skipped down the aisle, beaming from ear to ear, Annie keeping perfect pace with her.

Then it was Lauren's turn. But before she departed, she turned to Zoe who stood beside her bemused father. "You look beautiful."

"Really?'"

"Really. I'm so happy for you and Chris."

"Thanks. Me too." Zoe beamed.

Lauren glided toward the front of the church, smiling at Chris. He looked proud and happy to be standing in the groom's position, Mitch now his best man.

Then it was Zoe's turn, who walked sedately down the aisle. Lauren wondered if she was also heeding Celeste's advice not to gallop, but then she did a little quickstep just before she reached Chris.

Zoe's voice was filled with emotion as she spoke her vows – Chris's was, too. When Father Mike declared them man and wife and they kissed, Molly did a little jig.

"Yay!"

"Brrt!" *Double yay!*

"Definitely." Chris smiled at Molly and Annie.

The guests applauded as the newly married couples walked out of the church, preceded by Molly and Annie.

Claire and her husband collected Molly, thanking Zoe and Lauren once again, and saying they'd meet up with them at the reception.

Lauren's mother congratulated Zoe and Chris with a wry smile.

"Trust you to do something like this, Zoe. Congratulations, dear. I hope you two will be very happy together, just like Lauren and Mitch will be."

"Thanks, Aunt Celia." Zoe beamed. She looked up at Chris, her expression heartfelt. "Thank you for marrying me."

"I'm the one who should be thanking you," he murmured. "I've been wondering for a while what you would say if I proposed."

"If you'd asked me a few months ago, I mightn't have known either," she confessed softly. "But Lauren and Mitch inspired me to take a big leap."

"And I'll be here to catch you." Chris wrapped his arms around her. "Always remember that."

Once more tears came to Lauren's eyes.

Mitch's arm slipped around her waist. "And you know that I'll always be here for you. No matter what."

"I realized that a while ago." She looked up at him. "You'll have my heart forever."

"Brrt!" Annie approved.

Father Mike approached the two couples.

"Zoe, Chris, if you want to make it really legal, you'll have to get a marriage license and retake your vows."

"No problem." Zoe smiled, glancing up at Chris.

"We could do it next week," he offered.

"And have our own honeymoon right here in Gold Leaf Valley, while Lauren and Mitch jet off to Hawaii." Zoe giggled.

All the guests came over to congratulate them, making a big fuss of Annie as well. She preened, accepting the praise.

Lauren thanked Martha for arranging the senior center bus for their elderly guests.

"It was the least I could do." Martha winked at the five of them. "Here, Annie, here's your wedding gift from me." She held out a small, gaily wrapped parcel.

"Brrt?" Annie patted it with her paw. *Jingle.*

"Thank you," Lauren smiled. "I'm sure she'll love playing with it."

"Brrt!" *Yes!*

"And I've got a special present for you," Lauren spoke to her fur baby. "It should be arriving when Mitch and I are in Hawaii, so Zoe is going to mind it until we get back, and then we can open it together."

"Brrt!" *Thank you!*

It was a triple story cat platform. Annie had wanted to donate the value of her co-maid of honor gift to the animal shelter, and Lauren had honored her wishes. But she didn't want her fur baby to be left out.

"Lauren, your wedding was lovely." Mrs. Finch tapped her way over to them. "Yours too, Zoe." She shook her head in amusement.

"We'll be over at your house for craft club in two weeks' time," Lauren promised.

"And I'll drop in to visit you next week," Zoe added.

"Brrt!" *Me too!*

"Now it's time to take the photos, then have fun at the reception." Zoe's eyes lit up. "Lauren and I delivered her – ours now, I guess – cupcake tower this morning to the bistro, and it looks amazing!"

"There are plenty of cupcakes for everyone," Lauren assured Mrs. Finch.

"Chris and I will go halves with Aunt Celia for the wedding expenses." Zoe turned to Lauren, her tone serious. "And Mitch's parents for the rehearsal dinner. It's the right thing to do." She sounded like she wouldn't take no for an answer. "I know Mom and Dad put some money aside a while ago for my future wedding – they're probably relieved right now that it will finally be put to good use – our joint ceremony!" She beamed at her cousin, then at her parents, who stood nearby, still looking a little bemused. Lauren couldn't blame them, although she thought they must be used to Zoe's impulsive ideas by now.

The photographer directed them to stand next to a scarlet oak, the red and brown leaves a picturesque backdrop for their photos.

"There's only one thing left we have to do," Zoe announced.

"What's that?" Lauren asked.

"Make sure our waltzing practice pays off at the reception!"

"Brrt!"

THE END

I hope you enjoyed reading this mystery. Sign up to my newsletter at **www.JintyJames.com** and be among the first to discover when my next book is published!

Please turn the page for a list of all my books.

TITLES BY JINTY JAMES

Purrs and Peril – A Norwegian Forest Cat Café Cozy Mystery – Book 1

Meow Means Murder – A Norwegian Forest Cat Café Cozy Mystery – Book 2

Whiskers and Warrants – A Norwegian Forest Cat Café Cozy Mystery – Book 3

Two Tailed Trouble – A Norwegian Forest Cat Café Cozy Mystery – Book 4

Paws and Punishment – A Norwegian Forest Cat Café Cozy Mystery – Book 5

Kitty Cats and Crime – A Norwegian Forest Cat Café Cozy Mystery – Book 6

Catnaps and Clues – A
Norwegian Forest Cat Café Cozy
Mystery – Book 7

Pedigrees and Poison – A
Norwegian Forest Cat Café Cozy
Mystery – Book 8

Christmas Claws – A Norwegian
Forest Cat Café Cozy Mystery –
Book 9

Fur and Felons – A Norwegian
Forest Cat Café Cozy Mystery –
Book 10

Catmint and Crooks – A
Norwegian Forest Cat Café Cozy
Mystery – Book 11

Kittens and Killers – A
Norwegian Forest Cat Café Cozy
Mystery – Book 12

Felines and Footprints – A
Norwegian Forest Cat Café Cozy
Mystery – Book 13

Pouncing on the Proof – A Norwegian Forest Cat Café Cozy Mystery – Book 14

<u>Maddie Goodwell Series (fun witch cozies)</u>

Spells and Spiced Latte - A Coffee Witch Cozy Mystery - Maddie Goodwell

Visions and Vanilla Cappuccino - A Coffee Witch Cozy Mystery - Maddie Goodwell 2

Magic and Mocha – A Coffee Witch Cozy Mystery – Maddie Goodwell 3

Enchantments and Espresso – A Coffee Witch Cozy Mystery – Maddie Goodwell 4

Familiars and French Roast - A Coffee Witch Cozy Mystery – Maddie Goodwell 5

Incantations and Iced Coffee – A Coffee Witch Cozy Mystery – Maddie Goodwell 6

Printed in Great Britain
by Amazon

28072205R00139